At the mercy of . . . lust

She watched him undress, feeling the breeze caress her body. He was slim and well-muscled, his body bearing scars made by bullets and knives. When he removed his pants, her eyes widened as she saw his penis, swollen and pulsing. It was the first time she had ever seen a man . . . like that!

He turned to face her, giving her time to look at him fully before he approached her. Time to change her mind before they went too far.

At that point, however, she didn't really have any control over what would happen. She was entirely in his hands.

ANGEL EYES

ANGEL EYES

#1

THE MIRACLE OF REVENGE

Also by Robert J. Randisi

Angel Eyes

Tracker

Mountain Jack Pike

ANGEL EYES

#1

THE MIRACLE OF REVENGE

Robert J. Randisi

SPEAKING VOLUMES, LLC

NAPLES, FLORIDA

2012

ANGEL EYES

#1 THE MIRACLE OF REVENGE

ISBN 978-1-61232-583-5

For all the women of the world who have Angel Eyes
— and isn't that all of you?

PART ONE

CHAPTER ONE

ELIZABETH ARCHER was very tired and ravenously hungry. She had eaten the last of her meager food stores just before crossing the border from Kansas into Missouri, and that had been some time yesterday. She had no idea how far she was from the next town, but hoped that it wasn't too far. Actually, it didn't really matter because she had very little money with which to buy supplies, anyway. All she had left was some coffee and dried beef jerky.

For the thousandth time since leaving her home in Newton, Kansas, she touched her father's large Walker Colt. It was the gun she had used to kill Bill Nolan, and she had not fired it before that. Or since. She knew that if she had intentions of killing the rest of the Nolans, especially Les, she was going to have to practice firing the big gun. This time with her eyes open.

She urged her big bay mare, Blossom, forward because

she knew that if she stopped to think about what she had to do she would probably dissolve into tears and die. The trick was to deaden her senses and try not to think about it. The trick was to just go and do it.

Later, as darkness was drawing near, there was still no town in sight. The land was flat enough so that if there were any structures at all within a few miles, whether a single house or a town, she knew that she would be able to see them.

There were none.

There *was* something in the air, however, that gave her some hope of finding shelter, sustenance, or both. It hung in the air reminding her of the hunger that was eating at her belly.

What she smelled was the odor of something cooking. The strongest identifiable odors were of frying bacon and coffee, and they were causing her stomach to act up even more. Even Blossom was getting skittish.

"It's all right, Blossom," she said to the mare, patting her neck, "let's follow our noses and see what we can find."

She was hoping for at least a small house with friendly people who would invite her in. Perhaps it was hidden in a small valley and could not be seen from where she was.

She was worried about the cloak of darkness that was very quickly falling, but when it finally came it aided her. She was able to make out the glow of a campfire and made for it, relieved at finally having a definite destination in sight.

As she approached the campfire, however, she remembered something her father had told her brother about not riding into a stranger's camp without first calling out. Naturally, her father saw no reason to give his daughter the same advice, but she had been sitting nearby when he said it, and remembered it.

"Hello, the fire!" she called, reining Blossom in and listening intently for an answer.

"Come ahead," a man's voice called back.

She was immediately apprehensive about riding into a camp where there might be one man or more, but hunger overcame her fear, although she did keep her hand on the butt of the big Colt as she directed Blossom into the camp.

There was only one man that she could see, and he was standing by the fire cooking. Off to one side she could make out what appeared to be a peddler's wagon and three horses.

The man was about thirty-five or so, she guessed, tall and slim, but powerful-looking. He was clean-shaven and had a pleasant face, and she wondered about a man who would keep himself cleanly shaven even though he was on the trail. She could see that he was wondering about her, also. Apparently he approved of what he was seeing, for he was smiling.

"Hello," he said when she had ridden close enough for him to speak without shouting.

"Howdy," she replied. She was unsure of what to do next, so she waited.

"Step down off that mare, girl, before you fall off," the man finally said. "You look like you could use some food."

"That's the truth," she answered, dismounting wearily. "I ran out of supplies a ways back and was hoping to come across a town."

"Nearest town is a half day's ride from here. It's lucky for you we crossed trails. Sit and make yourself at home. I've got plenty."

"Thank you." She started to sit by the fire, then stopped short and said, "My horse . . ."

"You sit there and start eating, little lady. I'll take care of your horse. She looks like she could use a feedbag and some rest. You'll spend the night here, of course."

She stared at him, wondering exactly what he meant.

"You can sleep in my wagon," he said, with a grin, "and I'll sleep outside. What could be safer than that? In the morning I'll give you directions to the nearest town."

She still appeared a little apprehensive so he laughed and said, "Go ahead and eat. I'm not that bad a cook."

She began to eat while he cared for her horse. She watched as he unsaddled her mare and rubbed it down. She admired the gentle touch he used on Blossom. The man obviously had a good feel for horses.

When he had the mare staked out next to a good-looking gelding, making sure she had enough to feed on, he walked back to the fire to join her for dinner.

"That's a pretty bay you've got there," he complimented her. "Has she got a name?"

"Blossom."

"Blossom," he repeated. "That's a pretty name. How about you? Have you got a name?"

"Elizabeth," she answered, then added, "Liz — Liz Archer."

"Now there's a real pretty name," he said, putting a portion of bacon and beans onto a tin plate for himself. "Much too pretty to be shortened."

"I prefer Liz."

"Then I'll call you Liz, and you can call me Tate."

"Tate . . . what?"

"Tate Gilmore." He looked hard at her as if he expected her to recognize the name, but didn't seem disappointed when she did not.

She finished what she had in her plate and cast a coveting glance at what remained in the pan.

"Go ahead," he told her. "Take more. I've got plenty."

"Are you sure?"

"Eat it," he insisted, "and have some coffee."

She took what was left in the pan while he poured them both a cup of coffee. He watched while she finished it off quickly, as if afraid that he might change his mind and take it back.

"Guess you were pretty hungry," he said after she'd finished.

"I guess it showed, huh?" she asked sheepishly.

She picked up her coffee cup and drained it, then said, "I guess it wasn't very ladylike, wolfing my food down like that."

"Don't worry about that. I know what it's like to have an empty belly, and I know the joy of filling it up."

She studied him critically, noticing the numerous scars on his hands and face, and the leanness of his very tall form. He had been through a lot in his lifetime — which might have been longer than the thirty-five years she had first figured. She was suddenly very aware that her golden hair was dirty, and that she badly needed a bath.

Liz insisted on cleaning the tin plates and, after they each had another cup of coffee in their hands, Tate finally asked the questions she'd been waiting for: Where was she from, and where was she headed?

She had already decided, even before he asked, that she would tell him the truth. In spite of the fact that he was a stranger, she felt comfortable with Tate. She wanted to tell the truth.

"I'm hunting."

"Hunting?" he repeated. "Hunting what?"

"Some men," she said, and then went on before he had

time to make a joke about how she was too pretty to have to hunt for men. "They killed my family, and I'm going to kill them."

He stared at her for a few moments, then his eyes moved from her face down over her full breasts to her waist. She started to wonder if maybe she'd been wrong about him, but then he asked, "With that?" and she realized that he had been looking at the gun in her belt.

She looked down at it herself, then back at him and said, "Yes."

"Have you used it, yet?" he asked, putting his hand out for it. She hesitated, then took it out and handed it to him.

"I've used it," she said while he inspected it. "I've killed a man with it."

Tate looked at her and she wondered if he thought she was lying.

"I think I'd like to hear this story from the beginning," he finally said, "if you don't mind."

She hadn't spoken to anyone about it since the death of her entire family.

She told him the story.

She was engaged to marry Jack Marshall, who lived on the ranch next to theirs, she told him. They had grown up together and, as far as her father, mother and brother were concerned, he was already as much a part of the family as she was. It seemed only natural that they should get married.

One day, while she and her mother were working on her wedding dress, Jack went into town and never came back. The sheriff came to their house and told them that Jack had gotten into a gunfight with a gunslick named Bill Nolan, and he was dead.

"Jack wasn't no gunman!" she'd shouted at the sheriff. "That man murdered him!"

"Now, easy girl," Sheriff Ethan Lowe told her. "Get a hold on yourself. Your man and this Nolan got into an argument, and it ended up on the street, fair and square."

"That can't be!" she'd yelled, tears streaming down her face. "He can't be dead."

"He's dead, Liz," the sheriff said. "I'm sorry."

She cried in her mother's arms for a while, with her father's hand on her shoulder, and then went to her room.

"She has to be alone," her mother told her father, and they left her to herself.

First chance she had, while her family was out of the house, she grabbed her father's .44 Walker Colt, a gun much too big for her, and walked into town, looking for Bill Nolan.

She found him in the saloon. She knew it was him because he was still talking loudly about having killed that "little shit-kicker."

She held the .44 tightly in both hands, pointed it at Nolan's back and shouted to him to turn around.

"You killed my fiancé!" she screamed at him with tears stinging her eyes.

"Hell, little lady," Nolan said, smiling a broad, mocking smile, "what you gonna do with that big gun? It's much too heavy for you. 'Sides, I done you a favor, girl," he went on, moving toward her as he spoke. "That wasn't no man I shot down, that was a little pea —"

She closed her eyes right then, cocked the hammer and pulled the trigger of the big gun. The bullet struck Nolan in the right shoulder, spinning him around and sending him sprawling against the bar. The recoil from the shot knocked Liz back a few feet. Her wrists felt like they were broken, but she pulled back on the hammer again with both thumbs and held the gun steady.

"Shit," Nolan snapped, his eyes glazing over with pain, as Liz yanked on the trigger again, cocking and firing again . . . and again . . . and again until the hammer was falling on empty chambers.

Bill Nolan lay sprawled on the dusty saloon floor with three holes in him, and she had been lucky to hit him that many times. Luckily, the other shots had struck nothing but the floor and the walls.

Liz Archer walked over to the fallen man and stared down at him, the empty gun hanging limply from her fingertips. Then she turned and walked out.

When word got back to the sheriff, Liz Archer was not hard to find. She and her parents were at the funeral of her dead fiancé.

"Ethan," her father, Jim Archer, greeted the sheriff.

"Jim," Ethan Lowe said. "I guess you know why I'm here."

"Ain't hard to figure," Archer said. He touched the lawman's arm and said, "Ethan, you got to understand what the gal's been through."

"Jim," the sheriff said, cutting the man off gently, "I do understand, but I've still got to hold her."

"You can't put her in your jail," Jim Archer said. "You can't!"

Lowe looked over at the girl who was weeping on her mother's shoulder and rubbed his hand over his jaw.

"Look, Jim," he said, finally. "If you'll keep her on the ranch until the circuit judge arrives . . ."

"Thank you, Ethan," Liz Archer's father said. "Thank you."

"Yeah," Sheriff Ethan Lowe said. He looked at Liz Archer again and thought, a gal that pretty should never have to cry.

When the rest of the Nolan family — father Gus, and brothers Joe, Blue and Les — found out what happened, they left Texas and headed for Newton, Kansas.

Moments before the Nolans arrived at the Archer ranch, a week after the deaths of Jack Marshall and Bill Nolan, Liz Archer's mother, Amy, asked her to go down to the root cellar and fetch some spices for dinner.

Liz was in that root cellar when Les Nolan kicked in the front door of her home, and the Nolans opened fire on her family.

"Nobody here but an old man and woman, and a boy," she heard a gruff voice complain.

"Where's the girl, damn it?" another voice demanded. Liz held her breath.

"Don't know, pa. Should we look for her?"

"No, Les," Gus Nolan said, an idea dawning on him. "No, we ain't gonna look for her. Let her come back and find her family wiped out. Let her feel what it's like, and let her know that this was her fault." He hesitated, and then said, "Let *her* suffer. Come on, Joe. Come on, Blue. We're done here."

Liz stayed in that root cellar for a long time before finally deciding that it was safe to come up.

And then she wished she had never come up.

They were all dead. Her father, mother, and her eighteen-year-old baby brother, Danny. Dead — killed by the Nolans! Just like Jack was killed by a Nolan. She had avenged that death, and she would avenge these, as well.

As if in a trance, she moved about the house, packing clothes and supplies, forgetting that she was not supposed to leave the ranch, let alone leave town.

The last thing she took was her father's Walker Colt, the one she had used to kill Bill Nolan.

She'd kill the rest of them, too, with the same gun.

With a last look at her dead family she left the house. She saddled her prize possession, the bay mare she called Blossom, and left in search of the Nolans. She swore that she would never give up until they were all dead.

As she rode away from her home, Nolan's voice echoed in her mind, telling her that it was her fault. Some day he would know how it felt to lose his entire family — Les, Joe, and Blue would soon be dead.

He had listened without interruption and, when she finished, Tate asked, "Are you bound and determined to do this, Liz?"

She raised her chin up high, fighting tears, and replied, "Yes, I am."

"Well then, you'd better get some rest."

"Why?"

"Because in the morning I'm going to help you."

"How?"

"I'm going to teach you how to shoot, Liz."

He stood up without giving her back the gun. She asked for it and he said, "No, not with this. You'll break your wrists firing this. I've got something better for you. I'll show it to you in the morning. Right now I want you to get some rest."

She obeyed him and went to his wagon to go to sleep. When she was inside she understood how he was going to help her. Hanging on the wooden walls inside the wagon were guns, many different kinds of guns, as well as gunbelts. Tate was apparently some kind of salesman, or gunsmith, and he was going to show her how to use a gun correctly.

Suddenly, her quest did not seem so futile. She was so excited that she didn't think she would be able to rest calmly, but soon dreams of vengeance danced in her head and she fell fast asleep.

CHAPTER TWO

IN THE MORNING, after a breakfast Liz had insisted on cooking, Tate brought out a gun and gave it to her.

"It's a Colt Paterson, thirty-four caliber. Try it and see how it feels."

She took it and marvelled at how much lighter and smaller it was than her father's Colt, and said as much.

"It's smaller and lighter," he agreed, "but if you know how to use it, it can be just as deadly. If you like it it's yours, and I'll teach you how to use it."

"I don't know what to say."

"Say yes or no."

"Yes."

"Put this on, then," he said, holding a gunbelt out to her. "It goes with the gun."

After she had put it on, he said, "Now put the gun away and let's get started."

She holstered the gun as he set up some tin cans and bottles so that they could start drilling with the new weapon.

"The first thing you've got to learn is to hit what you want to hit without consciously aiming at it."

"What about drawing fast?" she asked, drawing the gun from the holster.

He put his hand out and covered the gun with it.

"Correction," he said, looking very serious. "The first thing you've got to learn is never — never! — take your gun out of your holster unless you intend to use it, or clean it. If you pull your gun, Liz, people can only assume that you intend to use it. Taking it out when you *don't* is a good way to get yourself killed."

"I'm sorry," she mumbled, replacing the gun in its holster.

"Don't be sorry," he said. "Just remember what I said and don't worry about a fast draw. That's not nearly as important as hitting what you're shooting at. I've seen a lot of quick men get killed because they missed their first shot."

"I understand."

"All right, then. Let's get started."

For the rest of the day Liz Archer fired at bottles, cans, trees, and rocks, always listening to what Tate was telling her, filing it away in her mind so she'd always remember.

Along the way she began to get the feeling that Tate Gilmore was much more than just a salesman, or a gunsmith. He seemed to know everything there was to know about guns. She thought it was odd, though, that he made her do all of the shooting and never once drew his own gun to *show* her how it was done.

At dinner that night she asked him about it.

"It's like I told you this afternoon, Liz," he explained. "I don't ever take my gun out if I don't have to. It's not a toy. I don't play; I don't shoot at targets. It's different with you because you're just starting. Don't worry about whether or not *I* can shoot. You just concentrate on learning to shoot yourself."

From that moment on she was sure that Tate must have been a magician with a gun, because he didn't need to prove himself to anyone. That was what she wanted to become.

After two days of constant practicing she started to hit her targets pretty regularly. It *was* easy, as he had kept telling her. "See it in your mind, and then point the gun as if it were your finger."

"You've got perfect reflexes and perfect eyes for this, Liz," Tate told her. "You're a natural."

On the third day, using some of his own clothing and some long tree limbs, he created a scarecrow in the shape of a man for her to shoot at. He even put a gunbelt on it, complete with gun in holster.

"When you're facing a man with a gun," he explained, "his eyes will tell you everything, but you can't concentrate solely on his eyes. You've got to *watch* his eyes, and his gun hand, and don't be distracted by anything else he does, or anything else that is happening around you." He stared at her hard and said, "Concentrate!"

He walked over to the scarecrow and poked his finger into the chest.

"This is where you want to hit him," he said. "Dead center." He spread his hands out to encompass the upper torso of the phony gunman and said, "This is the largest part of the body. Don't ever get fancy and think you can shoot for an arm, or a hand. Shoot for your biggest target, because you may only get one shot and it has to do the maximum amount of damage possible.''

He walked back to her, stood behind her and said, ''When I say 'Go,' draw and fire, and hit him dead center.''

She spread her feet, distributing her weight the way he had taught her, dropped her hand near her gun and waited, keeping her eyes on the chest of the scarecrow, describing the hit in her mind.

''Now!'' Tate shouted. She drew and fired and a piece of the scarecrow's ''head'' flew off.

''Put that gun in your holster and get ready!'' Tate snapped as she stared. ''Don't ever react to a miss like that.''

She put the gun away and got herself ready again, feeling her face flush with humiliation.

He kept her there most of the day, firing and reloading, firing again, until five out of six shots were striking the dummy in the chest.

''Tomorrow we'll try for six out of six,'' he said at the end of the day.

At the end of the week she was able to draw her gun from her holster, fire and hit what she was ''pointing'' at with consistency.

''Don't aim,'' he kept drumming into her. ''Point, as if the barrel of the gun were an extension of your finger.''

At the end of the week he was shaking his head at her in amazement.

''You're incredible,'' he said, ''and I shouldn't be telling you that. Don't ever think that you're so good you don't have to concentrate any more.''

''I understand.''

''I know you do,'' he said. ''Just remember it.''

"I will."

She remembered everything this amazing man had taught her during the past week, and she found herself enjoying it. She enjoyed being his "pupil" until she would start to think about how she was going to use the knowledge she had gained. That's when it wasn't so enjoyable.

That night as they ate dinner she watched him and wondered if she was attractive to him. She knew she was pretty — hell, she knew she was beautiful, with long, golden hair and a full figure. Men had been looking at her since she was fourteen.

"I've taught you all I can, Liz," he said, breaking into her thoughts.

"And I appreciate it, Tate."

"I know you do, honey, but I want to ask you to do something for me."

"What?" she asked, leaning forward and wrapping her arms around her knees.

"I want you to think hard about what you're planning to do. Killing a man is no fun, and it's not an easy thing to do. It can change your whole life."

"I've killed a man already," she reminded him. "Besides my life changed when the Nolans killed my family, and my . . . the boy I was supposed to marry."

"Honey, Les Nolan is a professional gunman. Even with what I've taught you, chances are he'll kill you before you can clear leather."

"I'm pretty fast, Tate."

He smiled at her and said, "I know you are, honey. Just do what I ask, okay? Think about it ? That's all I'm asking."

"All right, Tate," she said, just to appease him. "I'll think about it."

She went off to sit by herself after that and through the

silence her pain was almost audible. She thought she would burst from trying to keep it inside. Suddenly Tate was there next to her, his hand on her shoulder. It was strangely comforting to have him touch her, and her heart began to beat a little faster.

"Do you want to talk?" he asked.

She shook her head.

"Thanks, but no. If I talk about it, I might change my mind, and I can't do that."

"Would that be so bad?" he asked, massaging her shoulder. It felt good, and it made her nervous, too. She had not yet been with a man, and she knew that a man like Tate must have known a lot of women in his time.

If Jack was alive now, she wouldn't be a virgin, any more. She would be a married woman, and she and Jack would have —

"Hey," Tate called.

"What?" she asked, startled. "Oh, I'm sorry. My mind drifted."

"Liz, you have to try and forget, at least for a while," he said, gently rubbing her shoulder.

"It's hard," she said, unconsciously leaning into his touch, "so very hard."

He put his other hand on her other shoulder and said, "I could help you, Liz. I could help you forget, at least for tonight."

He cupped her face in his hand, leaned close to her and kissed her. She started at the touch of his lips and said, "No, please."

"Why not?" he asked. "What's wrong?"

"I'm not — I've never —"

"Never been with a man?" he asked, rubbing her arms up and down.

"N-no."

"It might be what you need, Liz. It might help you. A lot of women grow up after . . . after they *become* women."

Grow up, she thought. Was that what she needed to do in order to be successful, grow up?

"I c-can't," she stammered, nervously. He had her too flustered to talk straight.

"Let me try and help you," he said. His hand undid the top button of her shirt, and then the next, and she was helpless to stop him. She couldn't seem to move and her heart was pounding so that she was afraid he might hear it.

She was naked under her shirt and his hands found her breasts. Her skin seemed to be burning from within, and when he touched her nipples she felt them harden. She became disoriented.

"Oh, God. Tate, I can't — " she started to say, pulling away.

"Are you afraid?"

"Yes," she whispered, as if ashamed. She didn't think that what she was feeling was shame, though. She thought that perhaps this feeling that was so strange and new to her was . . . desire!

She *wanted* him to touch her!

"Do you trust me?" he asked.

"Y-yes."

"Then just relax. I won't hurt you."

His voice was so reassuring, his touch so gentle, his eyes so kind, that she tried to do as he said. She tried to relax.

He peeled her shirt down over her shoulders, baring her breasts, and allowing his palms to graze her distended nipples.

"All right?"

"Yes," she replied in a low whisper. It was *more* than all right, she realized. It was wonderful.

He leaned forward, cupping her breasts in his calloused hands, and kissed her again. He forced her mouth open and his tongue flicked over her lips and then found *her* tongue. Slowly his mouth moved to her cheek, her chin, and then over the smooth line of her neck. Her heart was still pounding, but she no longer felt like pulling away.

"Okay?"

"Mmm," she replied, lazily. Suddenly she felt as if she were floating, and there had never been anything like it before.

His mouth continued downward until he was kissing the soft, smooth upper flesh of her breasts.

"You're very beautiful, Liz," he told her.

She was about to reply when suddenly she felt his mouth capture her right nipple and she caught her breath. As he suckled it gently she began to breathe again, carefully, easily, not wanting to affect what he was doing.

His hands came up to slide the shirt completely off her, and she helped. She was nude to the waist now and he pushed her back very gently until she was lying on a blanket he had spread out for her to sleep on. When his hands moved to her trousers, she tensed up again and was immediately sorry.

"Okay," he told her, "it's okay." He placed one hand on her belly and went back to kissing her breasts.

After a few moments she relaxed and started to experience that floating sensation again.

"Just relax," he told her, and she obeyed.

He caressed her breasts with one hand while trying to remove her trousers with the other. He was having difficulty and she didn't want him to take his hand away from her breasts, so she started to help him. In a few seconds she was totally naked, and could barely recall taking her clothes off.

"I'm going to undress," he told her. She tensed up again and he added, "Is that all right with you?"

She hesitated, then said, "Yes, go ahead."

She watched him undress, feeling the lukewarm breeze caress her body. He was slim and well-muscled, his body bearing scars made by bullets and knives. When he removed his pants, her eyes widened as she saw his penis, swollen and pulsing. It was the first time she had ever seen a man . . . like that!

He turned to face her giving her time to look at him fully before he approached her. Time to change her mind before they went too far.

At that point, however, she didn't really have any control over what would happen. She was entirely in his hands.

When he lay down next to her she felt his penis brush her leg. It felt so hot and smooth that she wanted to touch it, but she was afraid.

He began to touch her again with his hands and mouth. While his lips teased her nipples, his left hand travelled over the soft swell of her belly, gently brushed the pale hair between her legs, and then went even lower.

Something happened then that she couldn't control. She crossed her legs convulsively and said, "No," almost without realizing it. Suddenly, she was very frightened.

"I'm sorry — "

"Don't be," he said. His reaction puzzled her. Why wasn't he angry?

"I'm not angry, Liz," he said, as if he'd read her mind. He continued to stroke her breasts and added, "It takes a little time, that's all."

"Yes," she said, closing her eyes to the touch of her hands again.

Slowly, beneath the ministrations of his gentle hands, she began to relax again. When she uncrossed her legs he said softly but firmly, "Be still, Liz."

Tate slid his hand down over her belly again, entwined his fingers in her dense pubic hair and touched the tips of his fingers to her vaginal lips. She tensed, but was determined not to close her legs on him again.

She closed her eyes as gradually, all of his attention began to center . . . *there*!

When his fingers entered her she suddenly felt as if her body were coming alive. As he finally touched her clitoris her hips jumped uncontrollably and she gasped. Her hands reached out blindly, as if seeking something to hold onto.

"Here," he said, taking her hand and guiding it to the fleshy column between his legs. She closed her hand around it and held on tight. It felt harder than she could ever have imagined, and so large!

He continued to manipulate her until she was near her first orgasm. She thought she was going to die from pleasure!

She was very close to coming when he whispered, "It's time."

"Time for what?" she gasped.

He gave her the tenderest look she had ever received and said, "You'll see."

He raised himself above her. He couldn't possibly . . . fit all of himself. . . .

When the swollen head of his cock probed at her she cried out involuntarily, "You can't — "

"Yes, I can."

"All of it?"

"Yes."

"Will it hurt?"

"I won't lie to you, Liz," he said. "It will hurt for a moment, but you'll forget it almost immediately."

Without waiting for her reply he entered her, sliding in inch by inch, and she had never felt anything like it. Her eyes widened and she opened her legs wider. He pushed even deeper and she cried out when he suddenly encountered resistance.

He stopped and stared into her face.

"This is where it will hurt."

"I don't care," she told him, "I don't care . . ."

He probed further, gently at first and then increasingly harder until finally he broke through and filled her totally.

It did hurt momentarily, but she was beyond caring about anything but how he felt inside of her. He seemed to swell even larger inside of her and she lost control. He began to take her with long, deep strokes and she fought to keep from crying out. Suddenly, she felt a great rush building up inside of her and she closed her eyes tightly and held onto him because she could have sworn her whole body was going to explode. And then it did!

"I never dreamed . . ." she said afterward as she lay in the crook of his arm.

"It gets better."

She closed her eyes, snuggled up against him and said, "Oh God, it couldn't."

He laughed softly and then looked down into her eyes, studying them intently.

"Well, you'll have one advantage over anyone you face with that gun."

"What?"

"They'll take one look into those angel eyes of yours,"

he replied, ''and never take you seriously — until it's too late.''

That was the first time anyone referred to her as "Angel Eyes." She had no idea that the name would remain with her for the rest of her life, more a part of her than the name she was born with.

CHAPTER THREE

THEY WENT their separate ways the morning after Tate had inadvertently christened her "Angel Eyes."

"Think about what I told you, Liz," he said as they faced each other for the last time, she on her horse and he seated on the seat of her wagon. "Change your mind, please, before it's too late."

"It's already too late, Tate. I'll never forget what you've done for me, though."

"Neither will I," he replied. "I only hope I wasn't wrong."

He reached behind him into the wagon and came out with something crumpled in his hand.

"This is something I picked up somewhere along the way which *I'll* never use. I want you to have it."

Frowning she extended her hand to accept the gift from him. She took it, opened it up and found that it was a bright orange bandana made of very smooth material.

"It's beautiful."

"It's silk," he said. "I'd never wear something like that, but you're beautiful enough to do it justice."

"Tate," she said, with tears in her eyes. He watched as she tied it around her neck and then smiled at him. "I'll always wear it."

"Remember me when you look at it," he said.

"I don't need this to remember you." She gave him her hand. He took it and squeezed it gently.

"Good luck, Angel Eyes."

She travelled toward the next town in Missouri, while he headed for the Missouri-Kansas border. Tate had given her some supplies and money so that she could buy clothes when she reached the next town, Clearwater. She tried not to think about what she'd do for money when that ran out.

She had to start her search somewhere and Missouri seemed to be the best bet since it was the closest neighboring state to Newton, Kansas. She figured, and Tate had agreed, that after killing her family the Nolans would want to get out of Kansas as soon as possible, and that meant Missouri.

It wasn't until two weeks after she had parted company with Tate Gilmore that she finally found a Nolan.

When she rode into Oberon, Missouri, she saw a horse in front of the saloon bearing an "N" brand. She reined Blossom in immediately and tied her to the post in front of the saloon.

As she entered the saloon she remembered the last time she had been in a saloon, weeks ago, when she had gripped her father's .44 Colt Walker in both hands, closed her eyes and fired at Billy Nolan.

This time, she vowed, her eyes would be wide open.

She was a strange sight as she walked through the bat-wing doors. It was not common for a confident young woman to be wearing a sidearm.

The fact that she was wearing a gun, coupled with the fact that she was a strikingly beautiful woman wearing a bright orange bandana caused all talk in the saloon to stop, and all eyes to fall on her.

She took advantage of the silence to ask, "Who owns that horse out front, with the 'N' brand?"

"I do," a man said, without hesitation.

She had intended to ask the owner what the 'N' stood for, but she could see by the man's face that he was a Nolan. The resemblance was unmistakable. He was eyeing her up and down, as were the other men in the place, and apparently he had no idea who she was. She knew him, though. He was a few years older than Billy Nolan had been, but the resemblance was uncanny.

"Which one are you?"

He grinned, looked at some of the other men and said, "Which one what?"

"Nolan. Which Nolan are you?"

He frowned now, growing puzzled, and said, "I'm Joe Nolan. What's it to you?"

"Joe Nolan," she repeated.

"That's right, honey," he said, looking amused now. He didn't use the word "honey" the way Tate Gilmore had used it. The way Joe Nolan said it made it sound like a dirty word.

"I've come to kill you," she told him.

The amused look on his face slipped only for a moment. "Is that a fact?" He pointed to the Colt Paterson on her hip and said, "You gonna use that little cannon on me?"

"I'll use this gun on you," she said, "but you may remember that I used a Colt Walker on your brother, Billy, back in Newton, Kansas, when I killed him."

Joe Nolan's face no longer looked amused as he pushed off the bar and stood up straight. He looked at her long blonde hair and frowned as he inspected her face, trying to remember if he'd ever seen her before. He hadn't, of course, but she knew that she must have been described to him at the time of his brother's death. She thought that recognition may have touched his face a bit.

"I'm going to give you a chance, Nolan," she said. "I'm going to let you draw."

Everyone in the room started to laugh except Joe Nolan, who wasn't sure if they were laughing at her or at him.

"Go ahead, pard," the bartender told him, laughing, "draw on this pretty lady with the angel eyes."

She heard the words "Angel Eyes" again, but she was too busy to pay attention to it. She remembered everything Tate had taught her and she was concentrating on Nolan's eyes, and his gun hand.

"Come on, Nolan," she said, backing away a bit. "Or are you afraid to draw on a woman?" Then she added, "The woman who killed your filthy little brother."

"You killed Billy!" Nolan said then, unsure of what he should do about it.

"I did," she admitted. "Now I'm going to kill you and the rest of your family, until all the Nolans are gone."

Nolan suddenly realized that he was going to have to stand up to this girl before the men in the saloon got the wrong idea.

"Little lady," he said, "you're gonna find it a little hard to kill the rest of the Nolans after I get through with you. If you're the little bitch who killed Billy, like you say, then

I'm gonna kill you, and enjoy it. But maybe I'll enjoy you a little, first.''

He started toward her and then suddenly went for his gun. It happened just like Tate had told her it would. She saw it in his eyes just before his hand moved, and as it moved it seemed to her to be moving in slow motion, so slow that she had all the time in the world to draw her own gun and fire the first shot.

She had her gun out before Nolan's had even cleared leather, and she put two neat holes in his chest, just the way Tate had taught her. She had cocked the hammer on the draw so that when she extended the gun in front of her and "pointed" it at Nolan all she had to do was pull the trigger. A split second after she had fired the first shot she cocked the hammer again and fired her second shot. You could have covered both holes with a playing card. Joe Nolan fell to the floor, as dead as his younger brother, Billy.

She decided not to wait around for the sheriff to come and ask questions. She had enough supplies with her from her previous stop so that she could ride right out of town.

She holstered her gun and looked around at the roomful of gaping men, whose looks alternated between her and the dead man on the floor.

"If the sheriff or anyone wants to know who killed him," she said to them all on the spur of the moment, "just tell them Angel Eyes."

She walked to the door, then turned and added, "Much obliged."

CHAPTER FOUR

IT WAS TWO MONTHS before Liz Archer — now known in Missouri as "Angel Eyes" — even picked up a hint of the Nolan scent again.

She had left Missouri a month and a half ago, but she still heard talk of the blonde girl with the orange bandana and lightning-fast gun. She had become something of a folk hero, without truly realizing it.

She was riding through Arkansas after Kansas, when she heard that a man named Les Nolan had killed a man in Fort Smith and been acquitted by Judge Parker. She found this strange because Judge Parker was known as "the Hanging Judge." How could a man kill another man, *in Fort Smith*, and not get hanged by Judge Parker?

That was the first inkling she had that the Nolans were something more than saddletramps and gunmen.

The first thing she noticed when she rode into Fort Smith was the courtyard outside the courthouse where the gallows stood. There were enough to accommodate a company of men to be hanged at one time. She shivered a little and rode past them to find a hotel.

During the past two months Liz had learned a lot about taking care of herself. When her money would run low she'd pick up an odd job, even if they were jobs normally done by men. She decided that she would do whatever she had to do to continue her search for the Nolans.

She had some money in her poke now, enough to stay a night in a hotel and maybe get a bath. Before either, though, she was going to put Blossom up at the livery and find out if Les Nolan was still in town. If he was she'd not waste any time bathing or taking a room, she'd kill him as soon as she found him. If he was not in Fort Smith, however, she'd take that room and bath, and start out in the morning to pick up his trail.

As she handed Blossom over to the liveryman she caught him looking at the orange bandana Tate had given her, and wondered if the stories about "Angel Eyes" had reached this far. Perhaps the man was simply looking at her the way all men looked at her, but she didn't want to take the chance. Before leaving the livery she tucked the bandana on the inside of her shirt collar, where it could not be seen.

The one thing a woman who looked like Liz Archer could not do was walk into a saloon without attracting attention, orange bandana or no, yet that was the best source of information in any town. Tucking her hair up into her hat, or down her collar to try and look like a boy wouldn't work because her body was so obviously female. She was going to have to try and find some way of drawing from that well of information *without* attracting too much attention.

Where else would a man like Les Nolan have stopped while in town? He had to have stayed in a hotel, so she decided to change her plans and go there first.

"Can I help you?" a young clerk asked eagerly, staring at her with unabashed admiration.

"Yes, I'd like a room."

"For how long?"

"Just the night."

"Yes, ma'am."

The man fumbled for a pen to hand her so she could sign the register, then turned the book around quickly so he could see her name.

"Miss Archer."

"That's right."

"Take room three, Miss Archer," he said, handing her the key. "It's the best room in the hotel."

"Any room will do," she said dejectedly, taking the key.

The clerk watched her walk up the steps until she was out of sight, wondering what could make such a pretty woman so sad.

What saddened her was that, according to the hotel registry, Les Nolan had checked out of the hotel yesterday, giving him more than a full day's head start on her. Considering she hadn't seen hide nor hair of a Nolan in a couple of months, that wasn't really too bad. Being less than a day-and-a-half behind one was actually the best she'd done in quite a while. She was here, so she might as well make the best of it, get a good night's rest, and a decent meal, and an early start in the morning. Maybe she could also find out why Nolan had been acquitted by Judge Parker after killing a man right in the Judge's lap.

When Judge Isaac Charles Parker had assumed his duties at Fort Smith he had been, at thirty-six, the youngest man on the federal bench. A year later that still held true.

During that first term of office, the former Missouri judge and Congressman had tried ninety-one criminals. Of eighteen murder cases, fifteen had ended in convictions. Out of eight killers sentenced to die on the gallows, one had been killed while trying to escape, one had had his sentence commuted to life, and the other six were hanged in public while thousands of spectators looked on.

Six men hanged in one year had earned him the nickname "the Hanging Judge," although, over the months, the number had grown every time someone told a Judge Parker story.

Resting in his rooms, Judge Parker was thinking about Les Nolan now. Nolan had escaped the Judge's gallows because there were witnesses who called it a fair fight. Isaac Parker *knew* that Les Nolan as good as killed that man and said so in court.

"You murdered that man, Nolan, as sure as you're standing here in my court, and I'd like nothing better than to sentence you to hang. I must abide by the law, though, because without the law there would be more of your kind walking around."

Les Nolan had simply stood and stared at the Judge, knowing that he was going to walk off scot-free, no matter what the man behind the bench said.

"There is one thing I can do, though," the Judge went on, undaunted by Nolan's offensive smirk, "and that is banish you from Fort Smith." The Judge leaned forward now and stared intently at Nolan while he said, "If I so much as smell your presence in my jurisdiction, Nolan, I swear by all that I hold dear that I'll find an excuse to hang you. Case dismissed!"

Nolan was still smirking as he walked out of Judge Parker's court, yet when morning came he was nowhere to be found in Fort Smith.

Still, that gave little satisfaction to the Judge. One had

gotten away, one that should have swung by the neck.

The Judge had a bad temper. Even he knew that. He hoped that the next poor devil who stood in front of his bench wouldn't have to pay the price for Les Nolan.

CHAPTER FIVE

WHEN LIZ WOKE UP she stared at the ceiling, unsure where she was. For a moment she thought she was back on the ranch in Kansas, only she couldn't smell breakfast cooking.

Then it came to her. She was on the trail of the Nolans, and this hotel room was just another stop along the way.

She sat up, took a moment to get her bearings and wipe the sleep from her eyes, and then realized that she was ravenously hungry. Looking out of the window she saw that it was still daylight, although late afternoon. She poured water from a pitcher into a basin, splashed it on her face, and then went out in search of dinner.

Downstairs she asked the clerk where she could get a good meal, and he gave her directions to what he called, "the nicest eatery in Fort Smith."

"As long as it's got good food."

The café he had told her about was on Garrison Street. As she entered she was afraid she would have to go elsewhere, it was so crowded.

"Hi," a young waitress said, approaching her with a smile.

"I guess the fella at the hotel was right," Liz commented.

"About what?"

"The food here *must* be good."

"It's better'n fair, that's for sure," the waitress said. "Do you want to wait for a table? Might be a while."

"I guess I'll find someplace else — "

"There's room over here," a man's voice called out, and both women turned in its direction. Liz saw a tall, solid-looking man sitting alone at a table.

"There's plenty of room here," he said again, smiling pleasantly, "if you don't mind sharing a table."

The waitress looked at Liz, who said, "Hell, I'm too hungry to mind."

"Suit yourself," the waitress said, no longer smiling.

Liz walked over to the table and sat opposite the man, who was still smiling.

"I can tell you what we have," the waitress said coldly, "or I can suggest — "

"The lady will have what I'm having," the man said, interrupting her.

The waitress gave him an even colder glance, then looked at Liz who said, "That'll be fine."

The waitress threw the man another withering look, then turned and went to the kitchen to fill Liz's order.

"What's wrong with her?" Liz asked.

"She doesn't like me."

Looking at the man Liz couldn't imagine why. In his late thirties and clean-shaven, he was attractive, even imposing. She guessed his height — even while he was seated — at well over six feet.

"What are you doing in this godforsaken place?" he asked her.

"Passing through," she replied, eyeing his plate of chicken and dumplings.

"I haven't started eating yet," he said, noticing her look. He lifted the plate and put it down in front of her. "You eat mine and I'll eat yours."

"Oh, I couldn't — " she started to protest.

"Of course you can, and you will. I insist."

She finally agreed, her hunger getting the better of her.

"I'll console myself with this," he said, lifting a glass with what looked like whiskey.

"They serve whiskey here?" she asked.

"They do for me," he said. He did not explain why, and she decided not to ask. He must have been a pretty important man in town.

When the waitress returned with Liz's order the man instructed her to put it in front of him, which she did with a bang.

"Wait," he told her as she turned to leave. To Liz he said, "Would you like some coffee?"

"Oh, yes."

"A pot of coffee and two cups," the man told the waitress, "and everything goes on my bill."

"Hey, Mister," Liz objected, "I can pay."

"So can I, and probably with less trouble than you," he said. "Please, allow me to do this. You're a guest in Fort Smith."

Liz thought it over and finally shrugged and said, "All right, if you want to that badly."

"I do."

They continued eating and Liz found it odd that he never asked her name, and never offered his. She decided to do the same.

When they had finished their coffee and he called for the check she said, "Thank you for the meal. It was delicious."

"It was my pleasure, I assure you," he said. She saw that he was studying her and guessed correctly that a question was coming.

"How old are you?" he finally asked.

Surprised, she answered honestly.

"Twenty-two."

"You look like you're either on the dodge, or on the hunt," he said. "I don't think I've ever seen that look on a woman before — not one so young, anyway."

She didn't reply.

"No comment? Well, I didn't expect one."

The waitress came and he paid the bill. Liz rose to leave first and he touched her arm, the first time he had put his hand on her.

"Whatever you're after, or who, be careful. You have youth and beauty, and it would be a shame for them both to go to waste."

"I've got something else, too."

"What's that?"

"A duty, to myself and to . . . others. When I've fulfilled that . . ."

"Yes," the man said, releasing her arm, "you will fulfill it. At what price?"

"Whatever the price is," she said, "I'll pay it gladly. Thank you for the meal, but I don't need your advice."

"You're welcome," he said, "for the meal. The

advice?'' He lifted his hands helplessly. ''Take it or leave it, as you wish.''

''I'll leave it,'' she answered, ''not because I wish, but because I must.''

He watched as she walked towards the door and said, ''We all have things we *must* do.''

After leaving the café, her hunger satisfied but not her curiosity, Liz decided that she wanted a drink before going back to the hotel for a bath.

She headed for the saloon.

She knew she was going to attract attention, but at this time of night the saloon was sure to be crowded, especially if it had gambling tables. Perhaps she'd be able to get in and out after one drink without having to repulse some cowboy's advances.

Sam Dewey saw the young blonde woman enter the saloon and make for the bar, and nudged the man next to him.

''How about that one, Styles?''

Pete Styles, a handsome young man who worked with Dewey and some of the other men at his table on a ranch near town, followed his companion's gaze and saw the girl.

''Oh, yes,'' he said.

''Oh, no,'' Dewey said, shaking his head. ''Not that one. Look at the way she wears that gun. She's more man than woman.''

''Look at the way she wears those pants,'' Styles countered. ''That one is all woman, and we all know that women respond to me. They can't help themselves.''

''I got twenty dollars that say this one can,'' Dewey said, challengingly.

"Hold the money, Claude," Styles said to one of the other men at the table.

He stood up, momentarily losing his balance drunkenly. Righting himself, Styles bore down on his target.

Liz decided on a beer, and the bartender, slightly taken aback, brought it to her and then looked directly over her shoulder. That look told her what was coming, and she hoped that the cowboy would take rejection gracefully.

Watching in the mirror behind the bar she saw a hand appear, then a shoulder, as the man tried to squeeze between her and the person next to her, a big, florid-faced cowboy who was only interested in drinking.

" 'Scuse me, Hoss," her would-be suitor said, elbowing the big man a bit. The big man turned and looked down at the handsome cowboy.

"Who you pushin', son?"

"Just tryin' to get to the bar, Hoss," the other man said, almost apologetically.

"The bar?" the big man said. Liz saw that he had a heavily lined face, broad shoulders and a belly that hung over his gunbelt. The cowboy who had been making his way over to her was short and slim with blonde hair and a handsome face. "You got a table, friend. What you want to get to the bar for? Me and my buddies wanted a table when we came here, but you had one, so we had to settle for the bar. You wanna give up your table?"

"No," the younger cowboy said, casting a nervous glance at Liz now, probably wondering what she was thinking about him. "No, me and my friends ain't givin' up our table."

"Then go on back to it," the big man said. His meaty

hands reached out and took hold of the smaller man, lifted him and threw him toward his table.

His friends, seeing Styles practically fly through the air towards them, scattered as he landed on the table. The table hit the floor, and so did the man.

"Goddamn pretty boy," said the big cowboy at the bar. The big man looked at Liz now and said, "You like pretty boys?"

She could smell the man's body odor, as well as his fetid breath, and said, "They're not really my type."

"Hah!"

"But I prefer them to huge, smelly, overgrown boys."

"What?"

Liz lifted her beer mug to drink some of what she paid for, but the big man slapped it out of her hands, sending it to the floor where it shattered into many pieces.

"Hey!"

Eyes turned toward the fallen man, but it was his friend Dewey, who had called out above the racket.

"You shoutin' at me?" the big man demanded.

"That's a lady, friend," Dewey said, stepping forward. "You don't treat a lady like that."

"I don't see no lady, *friend*," the other man said. "Why don't you come over here and show her to me."

"Look," Liz said to the man who had come to her defense, "I can fight my own battles."

"You just settle down, little lady," the man said, moving toward her, "and let ol' Dewey handle it for you."

Dewey was a little larger than his friend Styles, about the same age as well, but still no match for the larger man, who was itching for a fight with three or four men behind him.

But the big man did not have hand-to-hand in mind.

As Dewey approached Liz the bigger man suddenly drew his gun and fired. The bullet hit Dewey in the side. It drove through him, tearing through his heart and out the other side.

"Hey!" Styles shouted, because this had been more than he — or anyone else — had expected.

"You want some?" the big man asked, turning his gun towards him.

"There wasn't no need for that!" Styles shouted, looking at Dewey, who lay crumpled up on the floor.

"What's your name?" Liz Archer asked suddenly, and her voice seemed to have a calming effect on the situation.

The room fell silent and the big man said, "Are you talking to me lady?"

"Yes. What's your name?"

"Poole. What's it to ya?"

"I like to know a man's name before I kill him."

"What?" Poole asked, not sure he'd heard right. His gun was still pointing at Styles, because he naturally considered the man more of a threat than the woman.

"You heard me," Liz said. "Either put up that gun and wait for the law, or I'll kill you."

"The law? What the hell for? It was a fair fight. Everybody saw it."

"You murdered that man and you're going to answer to the law for it," Liz said, and suddenly she wasn't talking to a man named Poole, but one named Nolan.

"Lady, you're crazy. I got my gun out already, and your toy is in your holster. You better just take a walk before I take you and put you up on this bar and show you what a woman's for."

"You haven't got the nerve," she told him, "or the equipment."

"Lady," Poole said, and suddenly he swung his gun towards her, his face red with rage.

That was all she needed, the excuse. Her hand flashed toward her gun she watched his gun swing towards her. His hand was still moving when she pulled the trigger the first time, sending a hot chunk of lead searing through his ample belly.

"Wha — " Poole said, staring at her in disbelief. He wanted desperately to pull the trigger of his own gun, but the pain in his belly was far too great, and besides, his gun was getting heavy.

The man immediately behind Poole watched his friend fall and went for his own gun. Liz didn't hesitate a moment in pulling the trigger again. Tate's lessons had been well learned, for she never once thought about trying to shoot the man's gun from his hand. Her shot went straight into his chest. He coughed and fell to the floor.

"Anyone else?" she asked, eyeing the other men who had been with Poole.

"How about me?" a voice said from behind her.

"Who are you?" she asked, while keeping her eyes on Poole's friends.

"Federal Marshall, Lady," the voice said, "and I'll take that gun."

Liz chanced a quick look at Styles, who nodded to tell her that there was indeed a lawman behind her.

"Sure, Marshall," Angel Eyes said. "It's all yours."

CHAPTER SIX

THERE WAS quite a crowd to watch Liz Archer marched from the saloon to the jailhouse, among them a very interested spectator planning to take a personal interest in the proceedings.

Pete Styles accompanied the marshall, Leo Kelly. Kelly had Liz's gun tucked into his belt while his own gun remained holstered. He didn't really expect all that much trouble from a woman.

Pete Styles wasn't giving him much trouble either, except to insist that Liz had acted not only in self-defense, but to save *his* life as well.

Kelly, a tall, thin man in his early fifties, was bottom man on the totem pole of Judge Parker's marshalls, and was forever trying to work his way up.

"You don't have to tell the story to me, friend," the marshall told Styles. "Tell it to the Judge in the morning."

"Yeah, but then she's gotta spend the night in jail, and that ain't right."

"Maybe not, but the only other people I might stick in jail are dead. She's the only one left, and she's going — unless you want to go with her? Only you'd be in with the other inmates, while I'm going to have to find a nice, private cell for her."

Styles looked stricken at the idea of having to go to jail, and once again Liz Archer came to his rescue.

"Don't worry about it, cowboy," she said. "I'll survive."

Liz Archer had grown up a lot since she and Tate Gilmore had parted company, but she wished she felt as confident as she sounded that she could survive a night in jail. On top of that, there was always the possibility that they'd check her background. If they did, Sheriff Ethan Lowe would find out where she was, and she still had to answer for Joe Nolan.

When they reached the jailhouse the marshall told Styles, "This is as far as you go, cowboy, unless you want a room for the night."

"I just — "

"Go on home," Liz told him. "It's all right."

Styles watched while the marshall herded Liz inside, then reluctantly turned to go back to the saloon.

Inside, the marshall said, "Have a seat, Miss. I'll have to see about a cell for — "

The lawman was interrupted by the arrival of Sheriff Sutton.

"Sutton," Kelly said.

"Butting in again, eh, Kelly?" Sutton, a portly man in his late forties, resented Kelly's constant interference with his duties as town sheriff.

Kelly shrugged and said, "You weren't around when the shooting started, as usual, Sutton. Somebody had to step in."

"Still trying to butter the Judge up, huh, Kelly? Well, he wants to see you."

"Now?"

"Now — with the girl, in his chambers."

"Court ain't in session this late."

"Maybe court ain't," Sutton said, "but the Judge is."

"Who told him what was going on?" Kelly demanded, eyeing Sutton suspiciously.

"Nobody. He was passing by and saw you taking the girl out of the saloon. He wants to see you, Kelly. Now."

Kelly frowned, then looked at Liz Archer and said, "I don't know why the Judge is taking a personal interest in you, but let's not keep him waiting."

Liz, all for anything that would keep her out of a cell a little longer, got to her feet and accompanied the marshall and the sheriff to Judge Parker's chambers, across the compound.

When the two lawmen marched Liz into the Judge's presence, she stopped short and gaped at the man behind the desk.

"You!"

The man behind the desk smiled and said, "Not as pleasant a meeting as dinner, I daresay."

Kelly and Sutton exchanged puzzled glances, and then the Judge barked out, "You men can go. Kelly, wait outside until I call you."

"Yes, sir," both men said, and left the room.

"Take a seat, please," Parker invited her. "Sorry I have nothing to offer you."

"My freedom would be nice," Liz said, boldly.

He smiled at her, looking for all the world like a pleasant-faced banker rather than the infamous "Hanging Judge" Parker.

"You're surprised."

"Well, at least now I understand why the waitress didn't like you."

"A man in my position is hated more than liked. You learn to live with it."

"Is it worth it?"

Parker shrugged his broad shoulders and said, "If justice is served, that's my only concern."

"And in my case?"

"I knew you had that look," Parker said. "You killed two men tonight. Was that your intent?"

"It's my intent to kill some men," she admitted, "but not those two."

Parker frowned and said, "We'll pass over the men you do want to kill and talk about the two you did kill tonight. Would you like to tell me about it?"

Liz explained the incident that took place in the saloon, leading up to the death of three men, two by her hand. When she was finished Judge Parker bellowed for the marshall, who was in the room like a shot.

"Yessir?"

"Get me — what was his name?" he asked Liz.

"I think I heard someone call him Styles. He walked with us to the jailhouse."

"Get me that man."

"He may have gone back to — "

"Get him for me, Marshall!"

"Yessir."

"While we're waiting," Parker said as the marshall left, "would you like to tell me about the men you intend to kill?"

Liz hesitated a moment, then decided that the Judge certainly couldn't put her in jail for something she *intended* to do. She told him the story about the Nolans, admitting that she had killed Joe Nolan, and neglecting to mention that she had shot down Billy Nolan in Kansas.

"You're from Kansas?"

"Born and raised."

"You gave this man Joe Nolan a fair chance to draw?"

"Yes."

"What about Billy Nolan?"

Her surprise must have been evident on her face.

"It's my business to keep up on these matters, Elizabeth," he told her. "I suspect the sheriff of Newton, Kansas, would be interested in finding out your whereabouts."

Her heart sank. He knew her name, too.

"I got your name from the hotel register, and you *wrote* Newton, Kansas, there, as well. That was a little careless, but I guess you haven't been on the dodge long."

"Are you gonna tell him?" she asked, responding to the Judge's previous remark.

Before Parker could answer, the marshall returned with Pete Styles in tow.

"He was in the saloon," the lawman said.

Parker ignored him and asked, "Are you Pete Styles?"

"Yes, sir," Styles replied, nervously crushing his hat in his hands.

"Mr. Styles, I'd like you to tell me what transpired in the saloon earlier this evening."

"Huh?"

"What happened in the saloon?"

"Oh, yeah," Pete Styles said, and proceeded to tell the Judge basically the same story Liz had told minutes earlier, only from his point of view. He was even honest about his intentions when he first approached Liz.

"All right, Mr. Styles," Parker said when the man finished his story. "You can go."

"Thank you, sir."

"Thank you for coming and telling the truth."

Styles, throwing nervous glances towards Liz, said, "Hey, it was the least I could do. The lady saved my life."

"That's right," Parker said. "I guess she did. Marshall, you can go, too. Leave Miss Archer's gun."

"But Judge — "

"Marshall!"

The lawman took Liz's gun from his belt, set it on the Judge's desk, and he and Styles left.

"Is everybody afraid of you like that?"

"Either that, or they hate me."

"Your own men, too?"

"My own men especially," Parker said, smiling. "Pick up your gun, Elizabeth. You're free to go."

"I am?" Liz asked in surprise.

"You obviously acted in self-defense, and saved that young man's life, as well. I don't see any reason to hold you, do you?"

"No . . . sir, I don't."

"All right, then. I suspect you'll want to get some sleep, so that you can get an early start in the morning," he said, pointedly. "As charming a dinner companion as you are, I think you'll understand if I don't ask you to stay in Fort Smith for a while longer."

"Sure, Judge," she said, standing up. She walked to the Judge's desk, took her gun back and slipped it into her holster. "I understand, Judge. I was planning on leaving in the morning, anyway."

"Going after Les Nolan?"

"Yes."

"He's a dangerous man, Elizabeth," Parker warned her. "Better than a fair hand with a gun."

"So am I."

"So I've gathered," he said, sitting back and studying her. "Please, remember what I said to you in the café. It still applies, perhaps even more so."

"I'll remember, Judge," she said, starting for the door. As she reached it she turned and looked at the man behind the desk and said, "Thank you."

"Don't thank me," Parker said. "If I was smart I'd leave you in a cell for a few days until Nolan's trail was cold, for your own good."

She smiled at him then and said, "You know what?"

"What?"

"I don't think you're all that frightening."

He smiled back at her and said, "Neither do I, but let's not tell anyone. All right?"

CHAPTER SEVEN

LES NOLAN DISAPPEARED.

That is, his trail did. It just seemed to dry up and blow away. Of course, an experienced tracker might have been able to pick it up, but that wasn't the kind of trail she was following. Her trail was the word of mouth kind, from town to town. She had been following it for a month until it led her to the town of Kingdom Come, Louisiana.

It troubled her that Les Nolan had been able to stay ahead of her for so long, even though she'd been less than two days behind him after leaving Fort Smith. Now he was gone, damn him!

Where?

Had he known she was following him? Had he been stringing her along until he got bored? No! He was, after all, a Nolan—and a man. If he knew that a woman was on his trail, the woman who had killed two of his brothers, he would have turned and waited for her, and killed her. Or tried to.

Maybe that was what she should have done. Send telegrams up ahead to let him know that she was coming. Maybe he was still up ahead of her somewhere. If she sent those telegrams now, would it do any good?

That was a laugh, she thought, approaching Kingdom Come. Send a telegram? She didn't even have enough money left to pay for a hotel or a decent meal. She was going to have to find a job in order to survive, in order to keep going. Nolan's trail may have been cold, but she wasn't giving up. She'd keep zig-zagging across the west if she had to, until she crossed a Nolan trail again, and when she did she'd be ready.

More than ready!

PART TWO

CHAPTER EIGHT

KINGDOM COME was not a large town, although it appeared to have its share of hustle and bustle early in the day. Liz hoped that it would be large enough for her to find a job fairly easily.

She found the livery stable, hoping that the liveryman would not demand some degree of payment in advance. She hated to do it, but she used his obvious interest in her to get away without payment. He gave her directions to the hotel and promised to take good care of Blossom.

She went to the hotel to register and the clerk, a man in his forties, duplicated the liveryman's interest with the same results.

In the safety of her room she sat and breathed easier. Blossom was taken care of and she had a room. A job was next on her list, so she'd be able to pay for everything.

She spent the last of her money on food, except for the price of a beer, and then went job hunting with little success.

Jobs were scarce; any open positions were for men. No matter how much she talked she couldn't get anyone to take a chance on her.

Beer was an acquired taste for Liz since taking up her search for the Nolans. She found that nothing else cut trail dust as well. She decided to go and get that last beer, to cry in, if for nothing else.

It was early in the day when she entered the Lady Louisa saloon and found it inhabited by only two people. She was grateful for that. At least she'd be able to sit and enjoy her final brew.

Seated at the rear table was Andrea Blake, called Andy by her friends and Lady Louisa by her customers. She was the "Lady Louisa" for whom the establishment was named and the owner. She originally had intended to call it Andy's Place, but since she was supplying girls as well as liquor, she wanted a more feminine name.

Catering to two of man's most basic needs—or wants— Andy figured she would have a gold mine on her hands. Only things hadn't worked out quite that way.

Andy Blake had been a popular whore in her day, but years had gone by, and pounds had come on, and now she was reduced to being a top Madame. Unfortunately, she did not have any special girls with which to entice the customers. Oh, she had girls, but so far Selene, Denise and Holly had not been able to attract the attention of her customers away from gambling on a consistent basis.

Seated at *her* table in *her* place, Andy Blake knew she needed the genuine article, the real thing, in order to make this place pay. As she looked up, into her life walked Liz Archer.

Seated at the other table, thirty-three-year-old Charles Edward Taker — known to his friends and enemies alike as "Chance" because he took so many — sat playing solitaire, waiting for a sucker to enter Lady Louisa's. He had spent the previous night with one of the establishment's young ladies, and it had been a singularly unmemorable experience. In fact, his stay in Kingdom Come had been a string of unmemorable days and nights. What the handsome gambler needed was something "special," something that would make getting up each morning worthwhile.

He heard the batwing doors swing open, looked up expectantly — hoping for a sucker, when Liz Archer entered *his* life.

CHAPTER NINE

As Liz ordered her beer, a rather plump woman in her forties moved next to her at the bar. "This one's on the house, Ernie," she said to the bartender.

"Sure, Andy."

Liz looked at the woman, raised her mug, and said, "Thanks."

"You passing through?"

"That depends."

"On what?"

"On whether or not I can afford to stay," Liz said. Then she thought a moment and added, "Come to think of it, I can't even afford to pass through."

"Short on money?"

"All I had left was the cost of this beer which you've kindly saved me."

The woman turned her back to the bar leaning her elbows

behind her. Her face was heavily made up, but Liz could see that she had once been very attractive.

"You wouldn't be hungry, would you?"

"I had some soup."

"That's no kind of meal. Sit down and I'll have Ernie bring something out."

Liz frowned at the woman and asked, "Why?"

The woman smiled and said, "I've got a proposition for you, and whether you say yes or no, it's worth a meal for you to listen."

Liz thought a moment, felt the pangs of hunger still gnawing at her insides, shrugged and said, "Why not?"

"Ernie, get the young lady a meal and bring it to my table."

"Whatever you say, boss," Ernie said, giving Liz an admiring look before going off to obey.

"Come on," the woman said to Liz.

They walked to the table the woman had been occupying when Liz entered, and sat down.

"My name's Andy Blake, or 'Lady Louisa' to my customers. You can call me Andy."

"Liz Archer."

"What's a lovely girl like you doing riding around the country?"

"You said you had a proposition for me," Liz reminded Andy, ignoring her question.

"Right, none of my business. All right, then. My offer."

Liz sipped her beer, seemingly uninterested, but her ears perked up from the moment she heard the word "offer" — only she was afraid of the kind of job a woman like Andy Blake would have to offer.

"I've got a nice place here, Liz, don't you think?"

Liz looked around and said, "It's all right."

"You're right," Andy said. "It's nothing special . . . but you are. I saw that as soon as you walked in." Liz was about to protest when Andy added, "So did he."

"Who?"

"That man sitting over there? That's Chance Taker."

Liz laughed, looked at the man and said, "What's his name?"

Andy laughed with her and said, "His name's Charles Edward Taker, but everybody calls him Chance."

"Why?" Liz asked, looking away from him when he caught her eye.

"Because he's a gambler. He's also a lady's man, and he noticed you as soon as you walked in. Surely, you must be used to being noticed by now? It can't be something new."

"No, it's not," Liz admitted. "Men have been noticing me since I was fourteen."

"How do you feel about that?"

Liz shrugged and said, "I don't know."

"Come on, Elizabeth," Andy said, knowingly. "Don't tell me you've never used it to your advantage."

Liz thought of the liveryman and hotel clerk with some guilt and said, "No, I won't tell you that."

"All right, then," Andy said, "here's my offer. I want you to work for me."

"Here?"

"Here."

Liz waited a beat, sipped her beer and then asked, "Doing what?"

Andy spread her hands and said, "Whatever it takes."

"I don't understand."

Andy frowned, studied Liz, and decided that she was telling the truth.

"How old are you?"

"Twenty-two."

"Where'd you grow up?"

"Newton, Kansas."

"That explains it."

"Explains what?"

Ernie came out of the back with a steaming plate of steak and potatoes, and Andy said, "You eat and I'll explain."

While Liz consumed the food Ernie placed in front of her, "Lady Louisa" told her what "her girls" did.

"What do you think?" Andy asked.

Liz finished chewing what was in her mouth and said, "The steak is very tender."

"Well," Andy said, smiling wryly, "there won't be much more of it unless I can come up with something to turn my operation around."

"Me? I'm that something?"

"Elizabeth," Andy said, leaning forward, "you're lovely, but when I get finished with you, you'll be the most beautiful thing the west has ever seen. I'll teach you how to dress, how to use rouge, powder, everything!"

Liz poked at a potato.

"What do you think?"

"Andy, I appreciate the offer, and I do need a job badly, but — "

"But what, honey?"

"I don't think I could do . . . some of the things you say your girls do."

"You're not a virgin, are you?"

Liz thought of her one night with Tate and said, "No." She felt like she was lying.

"But you're not very experienced, are you?"

Liz looked into her plate and said, "No."

"Honey, that's nothing to be ashamed of," Andy said, touching Liz's hand.

"I'm sorry — " Liz said, indicating the remainder of the food.

"Oh, go ahead and finish eating. I told you the meal was yours no matter what. Maybe we can figure something out."

"Like what?"

"Well, let's see," Andy said, putting her chin in her hand and studying the lovely blonde. "Why don't you work here, let me fix you up and you don't have to do anything you don't want to do ?"

"What would I *have* to do?"

"Dress nice, mingle with the customers, serve some drinks — " Andy started to say something, then stopped short. "Add some class."

Liz took her last two bits out of her pocket and slapped it down on the table.

"Since that's all I've got, I guess I really don't have a choice."

"That's just my point, honey," Andy said. "You do have a choice — and you're making it."

Chance Taker watched as Liz Archer got up from Andy's table and left, tossing him a sideways glance which she quickly redirected when his gaze met hers. He wondered what had been discussed at the table, and then decided to find out.

He scooped up his cards — he was rarely without a deck in his hands — and walked over to "Lady Louisa's" table.

"Chance," Andy said as the gambler seated himself opposite her. "I guess you noticed her."

"How could I not? What went on over here?"

"Nosey, aren't you?"

"Very, darling," he replied, smiling his most winning smile.

"Ah, Chance, my love, when you smile like that I can't refuse you anything."

"Except going upstairs with me, you fraud."

Andy laughed, as she always did when Chance broached this subject, and said, "You don't want an old woman like me, Chance, dear."

"One of these days," he said, eyeing Andy's opulent curves, "I'll get you upstairs, and then we'll see. Now tell me what you and that extraordinary woman discussed. Me, I hope."

"Only fleetingly. Actually, I've hired her to work here."

"Her?" he asked, in surprise. "Here? As one of Lady Louisa's girls?"

"Not exactly," Andy said, and explained to Chance the terms of their agreement.

"How are the other girls going to feel?"

"They're business-minded ladies," Andy said. "They'll recognize why I want Liz around. She's class, Chance. You recognized that."

"No question."

"With her around I'll attract more customers, and once they're in here I can sell them *something*."

"You know what they're going to want, Andy," Chance warned her.

"That little lady looks like she can take care of herself, Chance," Andy said.

"Are you going to put her in a dress?"

"Naturally."

"You gonna make her take off her gun?"

"We didn't talk about that," Andy said, and then

frowned and asked, "Why, do you have some reason to think that will be a problem?"

"I'm no gunman, Andy, but I know when someone knows how to use one. You can tell by the way she wears it."

"That's interesting," Andy said, looking somewhere over his head.

"What is she doing in town, anyway?"

"She wouldn't say, and I didn't press. You don't think she's — "

"She's what?"

"An outlaw?"

"On the dodge, you mean?" Chance asked in an exaggerated whisper.

"Well, it's possible, isn't it?"

"Anything's possible, I suppose."

"I'm looking for class and a draw," Andy said, "not trouble."

"Don't worry, Andy," Chance said, grinning, "I'll be around to keep my eye on her."

"And your hands off."

"Like you said, this little lady looks like she can take care of herself," he reminded her, "so I guess that'll be up to her, won't it?"

CHAPTER TEN

THE FIRST NIGHT Andy took Liz upstairs and showed her the dress she wanted her to wear. It was pink, sequined, and cut daringly low in the bodice.

"It was mine, but I can't fit into it, any more. I want you to wear it."

Liz caught her breath and then said, "It's beautiful." She held the dress in front of her and looked in Andy's full-length mirror.

"Put it on, Liz, and then come downstairs."

"I don't know . . . ," Liz said haltingly. She had never worn anything remotely like this before in her life, and she was concerned about the low neckline.

She looked at Andy who, at five-foot-five, was about the same height as she was. Andy was wearing a blue gown, which was also low in the front, though not as daringly so, and her full breasts semed to be overflowing. She was too plump, Liz thought, for the dress, but she supposed that Andy had the name "Lady Louisa" to live up to.

What did *she* have to live up to?

"Put it on, honey," Andy said, patting her on the arm. "If you don't like the way you look, then don't come down in it." Andy pointed to her closet and said, "Find something else in there that you feel better about. I'll wait downstairs."

"All right."

After Andy left Liz went through the dresses in the closet. She was sure the older woman couldn't fit into most of them any more, and she realized that the pink gown was the most beautiful. She decided to try it on.

Andy had worked on Liz's face for some time, trying to find the right shadings to use on her cheeks, her eyes and her lips. Liz looked at herself in the mirror. With her face painted and her body tucked neatly into the gown, her first thought — without any trace of self-consciousness — was that she had never seen anyone so beautiful.

Her breasts, more than half exposed, were creamy white mounds of flesh, firm and smooth. Her neck was too long she thought, though she had never noticed it before. She traced the line of her neck with her hand, ran her fingers over the upper slopes of her breasts, then ran both hands down over her slim waist and full hips.

She slid her feet into the high-heeled shoes Andy found for her and almost fell before regaining her balance. She walked around for a few minutes. Holding the hem of the gown up, she examined her dark-stockinged legs — Andy's stockings — and the high-heeled shoes.

As a child she had seen saloon girls, and "harlots," as her father called them, and had always wondered how she would look dressed up like that.

Now she knew.

She was stunning!

But where was she going to put her gun?

Downstairs the piano was filling the room with lively music.

"Is she coming down?" Chance asked Andy, looking up at the head of the steps.

"She'll be down," Andy said, confidently. "I don't know when, or what she'll be wearing, but she'll be down."

"I just hope these yahoos don't mob her."

"They know the rules."

House rules were that customers made arrangements to go upstairs with one of the girls through Lady Louisa, and at no time approached the girls themselves.

"This is different, though," Chance reminded her. "She's special."

"I know that. If she's affected you this way, she must be."

"I don't — " Chance Taker started to say but stopped short when Liz Archer appeared at the head of the stairs.

She started down the stairs, walking very carefully. With each step she took, someone else noticed her. When she finally reached the foot of the steps the room had gone silent; even the piano player stopped to stare.

The other girls—Selene, Denise, and Holly—clustered by the bar and also watched as the "new girl" made her entrance.

As Andy approached Liz, she was pleased to see that her protégé *had* worn the clothes that she had selected for her.

"My God," she said to the young blonde woman, taking her hands, "you're absolutely beautiful."

"Thank you," Liz said shyly.

"You can say that again," Chance said.

Liz looked at him and it was the first time their eyes met for an extended period of time. She held his gaze boldly at first, and then demurely lowered her eyes.

"Just take it easy, honey," Andy told Liz, patting her hand. "Walk around a bit, talk to people. Nobody is gonna bite you."

Liz nodded and started towards the bar. As she did the piano started up again and, as if that was a prearranged signal, men bore down on "Lady Louisa" as a group, with one single purpose in mind.

CHAPTER ELEVEN

AT THE END of the first week Andy Blake was amazed. Liz Archer had not once gone upstairs with a customer, and yet business had almost doubled. All she could figure was that Liz was drawing them in. When they realized that they couldn't do anything but look at her and talk to her, they took one of the other girls upstairs and *pretended* it was her.

Chance Taker had Andy puzzled, as well. For most of the week he had spent his time taking her customers' money at the poker table. Their arrangement was that she would get twenty per cent of his winnings, which did not *exactly* make it a house game, but. . . .

What puzzled her, however, was that he had still not spoken to Liz, although Andy knew that he was smitten. She had seen that look in men's eyes before, although, never in Chance's.

An interesting situation.

Her frustration came from the fact that she could *not* get Liz to take a customer upstairs. Andy was convinced that Liz had the makings of the finest whore she had ever seen, but she couldn't get the younger woman to agree.

Also, Liz had told Andy that she felt naked without her gun, so the blonde had gone to the gunshop in town and, using part of her salary, had purchased a New Line .22 Colt, which she tucked into the top of the stocking of her right leg. This reinforced Andy's fear that Liz might have been on the dodge.

At the end of that first week, she decided to ask her about it.

Liz had finally agreed to move from the hotel into a vacant room on the second floor, and that was where Andy found her, dressing for the night's work. As Andy entered the room Liz was tucking the little gun securely into her stocking top.

"That's what I wanted to talk to you about," Andy said, at the same time admiring the shapeliness of Liz's leg. Her legs had once been like that. Well, maybe not *as* lovely, but very close.

"My leg?" Liz asked, noticing Andy's interest.

"No, the gun."

"Andy —"

"I'm sorry, Liz, but we didn't really agree that I wouldn't pry. I just backed off when I realized that you didn't want to talk about your past."

"I still don't."

"That may be, but I think I've got the right to know if I bought trouble when I hired you."

"I didn't ask for this job," Liz reminded the older woman.

"That's true, but you took it."

The two women exchanged steady glares for a few moments, but it was Andy who looked away first.

"Look, honey, I don't want to fight. I'd just like to know why you insist on having a gun on you. Are you on the run?"

"From the law, you mean?"

"Is there another kind?"

"Yes," Liz said. "I guess you could say I'm on the run. Or I was when I came to town. I was running after someone, and when I find them I intend to kill them."

"When you find them?" Andy repeated. "Does that mean you're leaving?"

"I'm certainly not going to stay here for the rest of my life," Liz said. "I've got a job to do."

"Revenge?"

"Yes."

"Is there anything I could say that would make you stay?" Andy asked. "Is there anything that *could* make you stay?"

Liz hesitated too long before saying, "No," and Andy noticed.

"How about a man?"

Liz looked away.

"Like Chance?"

"He hasn't even spoken to me," Liz said, and Andy knew that she was right. There *was* something there, on both sides. Then why were they staying away from each other?

"I think he's afraid of you."

"Afraid of *me*?"

"Aren't you afraid of him?" Andy asked gently.

"I'm not afraid of anyone."

"That's a lie," Andy said. "You're afraid of Chance Taker."

"What a ridiculous name!"

"You two should talk about it."

"Hah! When he wants to talk he takes Selene or Denise upstairs. I haven't seen him with Holly, but I wouldn't be surprised."

"Well, you know you've become a little unapproachable, and untouchable, since you've been here. Do you know what the customers call you?"

"What?"

"The Duchess."

"Why?"

"Because to them you're like royalty. They'd all like to touch you, Liz, but none of them want to soil you. They go upstairs with one of the other girls and pretend that they're with you."

"That's sick."

"No, it's not. It's your doing. When you finally decide that you will go upstairs with one of them — "

"I won't."

"If you do, none of them will take you up on it. They'd be afraid to, just like Chance is afraid to even talk to you."

Liz studied Andy for a few moments and then, her face softening, asked, "Do you really think he is? Afraid, I mean?"

"Honey, I know how to read a man's face. Believe me, he's afraid of you and he's afraid of himself."

Liz grinned mischievously now and said, "Maybe *I* should talk to *him*."

Andy smiled and agreed. "That might be the way to go."

Liz turned to look at herself in the mirror patting her hair into place. She faced Andy and said, "Well, I guess it's time to go to work."

CHAPTER TWELVE

FROM THAT NIGHT ON Liz would stop by Chance's table from time to time, bringing him drinks or just stopping to watch him play poker. On some occasions she'd rest a hand on his shoulder, or brush his arm with her hip. It got to the point where she was enjoying the game.

To the surprise of the other three girls, they all got to like Liz. In the case of Denise and Holly, they genuinely liked her. Selene liked Liz's refusal to go upstairs with the customers since it was adding to her own income. A stunning brunette, tall and svelte, she was what Andy called a "touch" below an ace.

It was that competitive spirit of Selene's that perked her interest in Chance Taker.

"What does she think she's doing?" Holly said to Liz one day during the second week. Holly was a short, busty redhead who made up in energy what she lacked in actual beauty. Men liked redheads, she had often said, because they wanted to see if the red hair went all the way down.

"She's just trying to compete against me, Holly, that's all," Liz said.

"But look at her."

Liz did, and saw Selene with both hands on Chance's shoulders, almost giving him a massage while he played.

"Doesn't that bother you?"

"Why should it? He's not my man," Liz replied. "You know that as much as anyone."

"Do I?" Holly asked, eyeing Liz now. "He hasn't touched one of us since the beginning of the week, when you started, uh, stalking him."

"Who says I'm stalking him?"

"Selene, and that's what she's doing now."

"She's welcome to try."

"God, I wish I was as beautiful as you, Liz," Holly said.

"Don't be silly," Liz said, playing the remark down. "You're lovely."

"I'm not, but thanks for saying so. No, I mean it, you're so beautiful that you don't have to worry about another girl going after your man."

"I told you, he's not my man."

"Don't worry," Holly said, grinning. "He will be."

Toward the end of the second week the situation between Liz and Chance suddenly changed.

A couple of strangers came into Lady Louisa's and walked straight to the bar. One was a big man, well over six feet tall and in excess of two hundred and fifty pounds; the other was a slim, good-looking man who just missed being six feet tall. Both men were in their early thirties.

They ordered whiskey, and that was when the big one suddenly noticed Liz.

"Judas Priest!" he exclaimed breathlessly. "Do you see that, Marty?"

"Lay off, Willie," Marty Kaneel said.

"Why?" Willie Sisk asked.

"Look at her. There's a roomful of men here and ain't one of them near her. That one's untouchable."

"Not no more, she ain't," Willie said. He finished his shot of whiskey with a flick of his wrist, and then left the bar to approach Liz, ignoring his friend's protests.

"Hey, little lady," he called out. Liz, who was standing alone, turned to face him as he reached out and took hold of her left arm with his big hand. Her arms seemed almost as thin as a twig in his grasp. He apparently didn't know his own strength, because he was hurting her.

"Let go of my arm, please."

"Oh, I'll let go, all right," Willie said, grinning lewdly, "as soon as you show me where your room is. You and me is gonna get acquainted."

"There are other girls here who would be happy to go with you," Liz said, wincing at the pain in her arm. "Just talk to Lady Louisa."

"I'm talking to you, bitch. Let's go upstairs." As he said that he tightened his hold even more and Liz gasped.

"Let go!" she shouted, and everyone turned to look.

No one actually saw him move, but as Liz was reaching for the New Line .22, suddenly Chance was there behind the man, reaching for his shoulder.

"Hey, friend," Chance said loudly. "The lady said let go."

Willie shrugged Chance's hand off and said, "Go away, friend. Me and the lady has got business."

"Is that so?"

"Yeah."

"I don't think so," Chance said, and reached for the man's shoulder again. He pulled, trying to turn the man around, only the big hulk wouldn't bulge.

"Turn around, damn you!" Chance shouted. When the man ignored him Chance reared back and punched the man in the right kidney.

Willie grunted in surprise and his grip on Liz's arm loosened enough for her to pull away. Ignoring her, however, he turned to face Chance, who was preparing to launch another punch. Later, after Liz had thought it over, she was sure the man could have avoided the punch, yet he allowed it to land on his jaw with a resounding thud.

And he stared, unfazed, at Chance Taker.

"Shit!" Chance said, and suddenly the big man swung a backhanded blow that caught Chance on the left side of the face and snapped his head back. The gambler ended up lying on top of a table between Holly and a customer, staring in awe at Willie, who was advancing on him.

"I'm gonna break ya in half," Willie said, his eyes gleaming feverishly.

"I don't think so," a voice said from behind the man and he stopped momentarily to look over his shoulder.

Liz Archer was standing there with the New Line held arm's length in front of her.

Willie stared for a moment. Suddenly he smiled and said, "What are you gonna do with that, lady?"

"I'm going to use it if you don't walk out that door."

"That toy ain't gonna hurt me," Willie said. "Besides, I don't think you want to use it."

"Try me," she said, her voice as rock steady as the hand holding the gun.

"Uh, Willie," the big man's friend said. "Look at her eyes. She'll use it."

Willie flicked his eyes over to his friend once, and then looked back at Liz.

"Yeah, I guess she would."

Marty walked over to Willie and wrapped both hands around one of his massive arms.

"Come on, Willie. If she empties that thing it might hurt a bit."

"Yeah," Willie said, still staring at Liz. "Yeah. Little lady, we're gonna talk again."

"I don't think so."

Willie grinned and said, "Count on it." He walked out ahead of his friend, Marty, without once looking in Chance's direction.

When the big man was gone Andy breathed a sigh of relief and hurried over to her star attraction.

"Are you all right?"

"Sure," Liz said, hiking her skirt so she could replace the gun, "but now you know why I carry the gun."

"Yeah," Andy said, looking at Liz's left arm, which still bore the marks of the man's huge hand.

"Chance," Liz said. She hurried over to the gambler, who was standing a bit unsteadily.

"Are you all right?" she asked, worriedly. His lip was bleeding and she attempted to dab it with her dress.

"I'm fine," he said, brushing her hand away. "I had everything under control. Why'd you butt in?"

"Butt in?"

"I was supposed to be helping you," he argued, wiping

the blood off his face with the back of his hand and examining it.

"He was going to tear you apart. What was I supposed to do, watch?"

"That's what any one of these other girls would have done," he said, "but not you. Oh, no!"

Liz frowned at him, trying to understand, and then did.

"Your pride is hurt."

"Pride be damned!"

"No, that's it, isn't it? *I* helped *you* and you resent it."

"Liz," Andy said in her ear, "not here. Too many people."

Liz, who knew little of tact, looked at Andy and said, "What?"

"Drop it, for now," the older woman advised.

"Look, just forget it," Chance said, angrily. He walked to the bar and said, "Ernie, give me a bottle."

"Chance, you're not gonna play and dr —" the bartender started to say, but the gambler cut him off angrily.

"Just give me the bottle, damn it!"

"Sure, Chance, sure."

"Come on," Andy said, taking Liz by the arm, "let's go upstairs. How's your arm?"

Liz looked down at her bruised arm, and realized that it hurt.

"Let's put something on it," Andy said tugging Liz toward the stairs.

They went up the steps to Andy's room, where she soaked a cloth in cold water and wrapped it around the bruised area.

"Can you move your fingers?"

"Sure," Liz said, doing so.

"Good, then it's not broken."

"I don't understand that man," Liz said in frustration. "I saved his neck!"

"You don't understand men, period, honey," Andy said, pouring cold water over the cloth. "I'm going to explain all about the male ego to you, and why chivalry doesn't work in reverse."

CHAPTER THIRTEEN

CHANCE TAKER came to Liz Archer's room during the night. He'd had a few drinks but he was not drunk, so he couldn't use that as an excuse.

Liz Archer was lying awake in her bed, her body tense, taut. The exchange with Chance that day had been the most words they'd said to each other since they'd met—or was "met" even the right word? There was something between them, ever since that first day.

At least, that's the way she felt. Did he, she wondered, feel the same way?

That question was keeping her awake.

Andy thought she heard the stairs creaking and, when she opened her door a crack and peeked out, she saw Chance moving toward Selene's door? No, Liz's door.

Smiling, she closed her door and went back to bed.

The knock was light, but insistent.

"Coming," she said, donning a dressing gown given to her by Andy.

When she opened the door and saw Chance she gasped, her heart pounding.

"Chance!" she said, surprised.

"Can I come in?" he asked and, as an afterthought, added, "Elizabeth."

"It's late, and I was — "

"Awake," he said, peering at her face intently. "Sleep shows on the face, especially on a woman's face, and you couldn't sleep any more than I could."

"No," she said, after a moment, "I couldn't." She backed away from the door and said, "Come in."

Chance entered closing the door behind him.

"Now what?" she asked.

"I came to explain something," he said, "to myself and to you, but words . . . get in the way sometimes."

With that he took three quick steps, took her by the shoulders and kissed her. She was stunned, but only for a moment. After that, she leaned against him and returned the kiss avidly.

"You feel it, too," she whispered.

"Yes," he said, "yes, damn it, I do. I've been trying to deny it, but I can't any more."

"I'm glad — " she started to say, but then he was kissing her again, pushing her back until she bumped into the bed.

He eased his hands beneath the dressing gown and tugged it off her shoulders. He pulled at the knot that held her nightgown closed and then slid his hands inside to cup her breasts. She felt her nipples harden against his palms as he squeezed her firm breasts, moving his lips to her neck. She was floating again, as she had with Tate, but this was different, better somehow . . . much better.

He lowered her down onto her bed and she watched him undress. His chest was smooth, without a trace of hair, and his belly was flat. He was not overly muscled, but to her he was beautiful, slim and strong.

Then he was next to her, his lips finding hers again, his hands roving over her body, bringing it alive. Instinctively she reached between them and closed her hand around his rigid penis, loving the way it felt, smooth and hard and incredibly hot.

"Oh, God, Chance," she said, tugging at him, bringing him closer. There was a fire between her legs and he had what she needed to quench it.

As he entered her she bit her lip and wrapped her arms around him.

"God, Liz, you're so beautiful," he said into her ear. "You're so hot."

"Darling," she said, closing her mouth over his while he took her in long, slow strokes, easing in and out of her. It had been a long time since Tate had made her aware of her body, of the *sensations* that it was possible for her to experience, but Chance was heightening her awareness with every move. It was better than she could ever have imagined.

Suddenly there it was, that rush that came from deep down inside of her, and she opened herself to it.

"Liz," Chance called her name, and she felt him swell inside of her, and then they exploded together.

"We've wasted a lot of time," Liz said later, laying her head on Chance's smooth, hard chest.

"I've wasted a lot of time," he said, tightening his arms around her.

"Why?" she asked, curiously.

"I didn't want to admit that I was in love."

She picked her head up quickly and said, "Are you, Chance? Really?"

He smiled at her and said, "From the moment I saw you, Duchess."

"You started that name?"

He laughed and said, "Why not? It fits you."

She kissed his chest, swirling her tongue around one of his nipples and said, "You know what? I like it when you say it."

"Duchess."

"I'm sorry if I hurt your ego downstairs."

"What?" he asked, and she looked at his face quickly to see if she had made him angry again.

"Andy explained to me about the male ego," she explained. "I shouldn't have butted in. You would have beat him."

"Honey," he said, holding her tight, "he would have torn me apart."

"Then you're not mad?"

"I could never be mad at you."

"I'm glad."

She sat up, lifted a leg over him and then mounted him as if he were a horse. She dangled her full breasts in his face and he teased and nipped at the nipples with his teeth and tongue.

"Mmmm," she moaned, lifting her hips so that his stiff erection could slide easily into her. It was the first time she'd ever been atop a man—she looked forward to many "firsts" with Chance—and she couldn't believe how far inside her he seemed to be. As she rode him she thought she could feel the swollen head of his penis between her breasts.

"Oh, Chance."

"Liz."

And then there was no more talk, just wild bucking and slapping together of bodies until once again they achieved completion together.

CHAPTER FOURTEEN

LIZ ARCHER WAS HAPPY — but she felt guilty.

Two months had gone by in Kingdom Come, Louisiana. When she was with Chance, she felt happier than she had ever been in her life.

When she was alone, however, she thought of her dead family, and she felt only guilt. She was supposed to be out hunting for their killers, not staying put in Louisiana with the man she loved. She didn't have any right to be in love, not while the Nolans, any of them, still lived.

So she was of two minds and she didn't know which way to go. Should she choose happiness. Or revenge?

"There's only one answer, Duchess," Chance told her when she approached him with her dilemma in the privacy of her bed.

"What?" she asked, feeling safe in the circle of his arms.

"If you only feel sad and guilty when you're alone we'll

have to fix it so that you're never alone again.''

She laughed and said, ''I don't think Andy will let you move in here.''

''Well, then, if she won't, you'll have to move in with me.''

''In the hotel?''

''We'll find someplace — after we're married.''

''Married?'' she exploded, shocked. It was literally the last thing she would have expected the gambler to say. ''Did I hear you right?''

''I don't know,'' he said, frowning. ''What did I say?''

''You asked me to marry you, I think.''

Chance continued to frown and then said, ''Yeah, that sounds about right.''

''Oh, Charles — ''

''There's just one thing, Duchess.''

''What?''

''What I do for a living.''

''You gamble.''

''That's right, I gamble. And there's nothing else I can do.''

''Oh, honey, I would never ask you to give that up.''

''Even if I asked you to give up working at Andy's?''

''I can do that,'' Liz said. ''It's not the same thing. I don't even want to work here.''

''Good, because I don't want you to. I don't want other men looking at you.''

''That suits me,'' she said, pressing her bare breasts against his chest, and her nose against his. She flicked her tongue over his lips and said, ''That suits me fine.''

''Honey, I'm happy for you, I really am,'' Andy said, hugging Liz. '' But I feel like I'm the one who's responsible for you and Chance.''

"You are, Andy, and I thank you for it," giving the older woman a hard squeeze and then releasing her.

"No, I mean that I have to warn you."

"About what?"

"About Chance, honey," Andy said, looking at Liz seriously. "About the kind of man he is."

"What can you tell me about Charles I don't already know?" Liz asked, frowning.

"He's a gambler, honey," Andy said. "Do you know what that really means? I'd be surprised if he didn't take a deck of cards to bed with him."

Liz laughed and said, "I can tell you from personal experience — "

"That's my point, Elizabeth," Andy said, interrupting her. "You have very little personal experience with men. Are you absolutely sure that you're doing the right thing?"

"Oh, Andy," Liz said, understanding now that her friend and benefactor was worried about her. She touched Andy's shoulder and said, "I'm very sure."

"Then all I can do is wish you the best of luck, honey, because I think you're going to have your hands full with that man."

"I'll handle him, Andy," Liz said, confidently. "Don't you worry about that."

Downstairs, Charles Edward Taker was involved in a poker game — which was not unusual — but he was losing — and that was. Chance didn't lose very often, but he knew from past experience that when he did, it usually lasted a while. Too long a while. Years ago he had learned how to head off a losing streak: by changing the odds.

That usually meant at least one deal from the bottom of the deck.

Chance was very good with cards. He could deal seconds with the best of them, but he hated to do it and he usually played an honest game.

Until he started to lose.

Like now.

"All right," he said, " let's see if we can't change our luck this time around." He started dealing the cards.

The man seated across from him was a professional gambler, as was Chance, but where Chance dressed the part, with dark suits and ruffled shirts, this man simply wore trail clothes.

That was Charles Edward Taker's undoing.

Liz Archer, dressed in *her* trail clothes and wearing her .34, was leaving Andy's room when she heard the shot.

"What the hell," Andy snapped, rushing out of her room. A shot in her place usually meant trouble. Liz, recalling that Chance was downstairs, hurried after her.

The scene that greeted them was not a pleasant one. The table where Chance had been playing had been overturned, and from beneath it they could see the protruding legs of a man wearing dark clothes. The other players were standing about, looking at each other nervously. The batwing doors were swinging back and forth, as if someone had just come in — or gone out.

"Oh, shit," Andy whispered.

"Chance!" Liz shouted, and hurried down the steps with Andy on her heels.

When she reached the table Liz grabbed it and tried to move it, but it wasn't until a couple of men stepped forward to help her that she did. Then she saw Chance. The front of his white, ruffled shirt was dark red.

"Who did it?" she asked. When no one answered she looked up at the faces of the men around her and shouted, "Who killed him?"

"Another player, Liz," a man named Cotten said. He was a regular customer.

"Who?"

"Said his name was Olden." Cotten gestured towards the batwing doors and said, "He just left."

Liz jumped to her feet, ignored the shouts of Andy and ran out of the saloon. She saw a man across the street starting to mount a horse and she shouted, "Olden!"

The man stopped and turned.

"You calling me, lady?"

He was a big man, with a worn holster and a big Navy Colt.

"Are you Olden?"

"That's right."

"Did you just kill a man inside?"

"I killed a tinhorn cardcheat."

"Liar!"

"Lady, if he was your man I'm sorry, but he was dealing seconds, and nobody does that to me."

He started to turn away as she stepped into the street, shouting, "Don't turn your back on me!"

The man froze, because the tone of her voice told him that she meant it. He turned slowly to face her, and she saw his eyes fall to her gun.

"You gonna use that gun?"

"I am."

"Then let's get to," he said, wearily. He had been through this enough times before to know he couldn't avoid it. "I've got places to go."

"The only place you're going, Mister," Angel Eyes said, slipping the orange bandana out from under her shirt collar, "is straight to hell."

The man knew better than to take anything for granted, so when he made his move it was his best.

It wasn't good enough.

The spectators who had rushed out of the saloon to watch all swore that they didn't see her hand move. Her gun was just there, and then it spoke twice. Little puffs of dust jumped up off Olden's shirt and he staggered back with a shocked look — his gun still in his holster.

"Damn," he said in a voice choked with blood as he fell against his horse and onto the street.

"The sheriff's downstairs, Liz," Andy said, entering her room. She had taken Liz there after the shooting to keep her away from the mob.

"Andy," she said, turning her tear-streaked face toward the older woman, "he was lying, wasn't he? The man I killed?"

Andy sighed and said, "I spoke to the other players, honey. They said Chance was losing. I'm sorry, but I've known him to deal a card or two off the deck to avoid a losing streak. That was just his way, he didn't see anything wrong with that." She shrugged and added, "This time he got caught."

Liz stared at Andy and suddenly the older woman saw a change come over her.

"It's an omen, then."

"What do you mean?"

"It wasn't meant to be. Chance and me, here, it just wasn't meant to be. I've got to keep going, now, finish what I started. I've got to find the Nolans."

"Nolans? Honey, I don't understand."

"I've got to leave, Andy. Now."

"But the sherriff — "

"I'll go out the window. I can't afford to talk to the sheriff. He might decide to hold me, check on me."

"You *are* on the run."

"It was a misunderstanding, like this one. Andy —"

"It's all right, honey," Andy said, putting her hand out. Liz took it and Andy pulled her to her feet. "Wait."

Andy went to her dresser and took something out of the top drawer.

"Take this."

"What is it?"

It was an envelope and as Liz took it, Andy said, "Five hundred dollars."

"Oh Andy, I can't."

"Have you got some money in your room?"

"Nothing near this amount."

"That's all right, I'll make more." Andy stepped forward and impulsively hugged the younger woman. "Now go, damn you. I'll stall the sheriff so you can saddle your horse and get going. Move!"

"Thanks, Andy, for everything."

"Don't thank me," Andy said. "I was selfish. I still say you have the makings of a first-rate whore. If you ever make it, let me know, will you?"

Liz tried to smile and said, "You'll be the first, Andy. The very first."

It had all happened too fast. One minute she was hugging Andy, telling her that she could handle Chance and now, scant hours later, she was riding away from Kingdom Come. How far ahead of the law?

She reined Blossom in for a blow and considered the objects she had around her neck.

One was the orange bandana she had gotten from Tate. It had become her good luck charm.

The other was a hunk of metal on a chain that she had

gotten from Chance. She remembered that he'd given it to her last night. Before he'd been killed.

"I've got nothing to give you but this," he'd said, handing it to her.

"What is it?"

"It's just a little something I picked up along the way," he'd said, and she remembered that those were almost the exact words Tate had used when he gave her the bandana.

She looked at the object and saw a miniature metal ace of spades with a small hole at the top for the chain. The workmanship was brilliant.

The death card, he'd said.

She tucked it back into her shirt and thought, How right you were, my love.

PART THREE

CHAPTER FIFTEEN

TEXAS.

LIZ ARCHER had never been to Texas, and she was so
impressed by the size and scope of it that she took the time
to see some of it. She also needed something to occupy
her mind, so she rode through the panhandle for a while,
then turned south to towns like Dallas, Fort Worth, Wich-
ita Falls, Abilene, Waco, Austin, and others. She found
jobs to keep her busy during the day. She only thought
about Chance Taker, her family and her young fiancé —
the man she'd *thought* she'd loved until she'd met Chance
— at night.

   She was in a small east-Texas town called Lufton, a full
two months after the death of Chance Taker and nearly
five months since she'd left Missouri, when she picked up
the Nolan trail again.

She had decided to spend some time in Lufton catching her breath. Everything she had done since Chance's death had been sort of "on the run," and she felt it was time to slow down and deal with it.

Liz admitted that there were many things about Chance she hadn't known. But she'd been in love, and if there was one thing she *had* learned, it was that when you were in love you wore blinders. You saw what you wanted to see, and the Chance Taker she *saw* had not been the whole man.

He'd been a *gambler*, but she had *not* known what that meant. It meant a life of taking risks, and that's what got him killed. Accepting his death would make things a lot easier for Liz Archer. And she could complete her obligation to her family and to herself.

She swore she would not allow herself to be sidetracked again, as she had in Kingdom Come.

It was in the saloon in Lufton that she heard some talk about an incident that had taken place in San Saba, a town located directly in the center of the state.

"Damnedest thing you ever did see," a man at the table nearest her was saying. "This tall mean-looking fella — he just shot this other fella down easy as you please. Bang! And it was all over." The man shook his head and added, "I swear I never see'd him touch his gun."

The man who was speaking was a grizzled old trail bum, gray-haired and watery-eyed. You saw the type in almost every saloon in every town, covered with a coat of trail dust. The man he was with was younger, a townsman who, for the last three days, had seemed to be trying to work up the courage to approach Liz.

"What was this fella's name?" he asked the older man, flicking his eyes over toward Liz as he did.

"Funny thing," the trail bum said. "A man that quick with a gun you'd think he had himself a big rep, but I never heard tell of him before that day. Nolan, his name was."

Liz's head snapped up as the old man said that, and she was out of her chair before she knew it. The younger man saw her striding purposefully towards his table and couldn't believe his luck. She was coming over to him!

The old man, on the other hand, had no idea what was going on when all of a sudden a hand came down heavily on his shoulder.

"What was that name you said?" she demanded.

The man looked over his shoulder, frowned and was shocked to see the lovely woman standing behind him.

"What?"

"The name you just mentioned, old man," Liz said testily. "What was it?"

"Nolan," the younger man said, eager to help and ever more anxious to attract Liz's attention. "He said the man's name was Nolan."

"What was his first name?"

Puzzled, the old man said, "I think I heard somebody call him 'Les.'"

Les Nolan!

"I knew it!" she said fiercely. Her instinct had told her she'd cross their trail in Texas, and here it was. She'd missed Nolan by a day and a half in Louisiana and then had been . . . distracted.

"How long ago was this?" she demanded.

"A little more than a week, I guess," the old man said. "Mebbe more, now that I think of it."

"San Saba?"

"That's right."

She took her hand off the man's shoulder and headed for the street.

"Can I help—" the younger man started to say, but she was gone before he could get any further.

"Son," the old man said, "that there is a lady with killin' on her mind."

"Really?"

The old man nodded sagely and said, "I seen that look enough times before, boy. You don't want to get mixed up with that one."

"She's so pretty," the younger man said. "Almost like an angel."

"Them's the ones you got to watch out for, boy," the old man said, wisely, "Them's the ones that's angels from hell."

Liz went directly to her hotel, checked out, lugged her gear to the livery where she saddled Blossom and headed for San Saba. She knew she had no chance of finding Les Nolan there, but at least she was on the trail again.

The hunt was on, and this time she'd see it through to the end. The end of the Nolans!

SAN SABA, TEXAS.

San Saba was a small town, but Liz was so excited it could easily have been San Francisco.

She had already decided on her course of action. She would ask the first man she saw about Les Nolan. There was no sense wasting any time.

As she reached the livery and dismounted, a lad of about seventeen stepped out and stopped short when he saw the blonde with the big bay mare.

"Hello," she said, walking toward him.

"Uh, hello," the boy said and Liz decided to unashamedly take advantage of the boy with a case of moon eyes.

"Quiet town."

"Yes, ma'am."

"Heard you had some excitement a few weeks ago, though."

"Yes, ma'am."

"Could you tell me about it?" she asked, standing close to him.

"Uh, yes, ma'am," he replied, his voice rising in pitch as she got closer. "Feller with a fast gun shot one of our local cowboys."

"Fella named Nolan?"

"Yes, ma'am."

"Did the sheriff get involved?"

"No, ma'am," the boy said, shaking his head. "That Nolan feller lit out of town right after, before the sheriff had a chance to leave his office. He come right back here and got his horse."

"Which way did he ride?"

"South."

"Do you have any idea where he was going?"

"I got a right good idea," he said. "He had another man with him —"

"Was his name Nolan?"

"I don't think so," the boy said, frowning. "They didn't look like brothers, or nothing. I think they was just riding together."

"You said you had an idea where they were heading?"

"Yes, ma'am. They was talking while they saddled their horses. The Nolan feller said it was time to head for a place where they could relax, and the other feller asked him if he meant Diablo City."

"Diablo City?" She had never heard of it. "Is that in Texas?"

"I asked after they left. The sheriff said it sure was, but he wasn't going anywhere near it."

"Why not?"

"He said a lot of lawmen had gone to Diablo City and not come back. He said he wasn't gonna be a name on that list."

"I see," Liz said, thoughtfully. "Diablo City. Where is it?"

He shrugged and said, "South, near the border, I think. I ain't sure." Suddenly he brightened and asked eagerly, "You want me to try and find out for you. It wouldn't be no trouble."

"No, that's okay," she said. She turned and prepared to mount Blossom again.

"Ain't you stayin'?" the lad asked, obviously disappointed.

"Not this time," she said, mounting up. She dug out two bits and tossed it to him. "Maybe next time."

Diablo City, she thought as she wheeled the mare around and headed south. A place for Nolan to relax.

A place for Nolan — all the Nolans — to die.

CHAPTER SIXTEEN

DIABLO CITY, TEXAS.

LES NOLAN WAS HOME.

For many people Diablo City, Texas, was a haven, a place to hide from the law, from a bounty hunter, from an unwanted "wife," or simply from the world in general. For the Nolans, it was home.

In fact, Diablo City had been "founded" twenty years ago by old Gus Nolan, and one of his sons, Blue, had been born there. The ranch outside of town was the only home any of them had known for those twenty years, and although Gus's sons spent most of their time travelling and raising hell, they usually ended up back home sooner or later.

Because he had been travelling for the past five months Les Nolan did not find out about the death of his brother Joe until he returned to the Big "N" Ranch. When his father informed him of this, he exploded in a rage so violent that even Gus backed away from him.

"Shot by a woman?" Les exclaimed. "Both of them?"

"That's the word we got," Blue said.

"I don't believe it!"

"Well, believe that Joe is dead," Gus Nolan said. "I had his body shipped home to prove that. He's buried up on the hill, next to your brother and your mother."

"Damn!" Les shouted, red-faced. "Who was she, this woman? Why didn't you go after her?" he demanded of his younger brother. The argument had raged in the family ever since Blue was old enough to pick up a gun: who was faster, the oldest brother, Les, or the youngest, Blue.

"Because I wouldn't let him!" Gus Nolan shouted back, regaining his composure after backing away from his oldest son's rage. "Don't be yellin' at your brother or your pa, boy!"

"Pa—" Les started, but he stopped, obviously fighting for control.

They were in the large parlor of the Nolan ranchhouse, which Gus Nolan had built with his bare hands, and Les walked over to the bar they had installed only five years earlier. He poured himself a stiff drink, downed it, and then turned to face his brother and his father.

"All right, let me have it again."

Gus explained what they knew, that a woman had ridden into Oberon, Missouri, confronted Joe in the saloon and outdrew him.

"How could that be? How could a woman outdraw Joe?"

"Joe was no great hand with a gun, son," Gus reminded him, "not like you and Blue."

"But a woman!" Les said. Then a stricken look came over his face and he said, "Pa—"

"I know," Gus said, with a disgusted look.

"Pa, the same woman?" Les went on. "That . . . girl in Newton?"

"It couldn't be," Blue said. "In Newton she couldn't even control her gun, they said."

"Well, maybe she's learned," Les said, putting his empty glass down and starting for the door.

"Where you going?" Gus demanded.

"Newton!"

"No!" Gus shouted, and Les stopped and turned.

Gus walked up to his oldest son and said, "Use your head, son. If she killed Joe in Missouri, then she ain't in Newton. She's hunting."

"Hunting?" Les said, frowning. "Us?"

"That's why Pa didn't let me go looking for her," Blue said, moving alongside his brother and father.

"Sooner or later," Gus said, looking at both of his sons, "she's gonna show up here. She's got to."

"And when she does," Les continued, "we'll be waiting for her."

"This time," Gus said, "we'll finish the job."

Camped outside of Diablo City, Liz Archer was staring down at the town, which showed a few scattered lights as the only signs of life. She was cleaning her gun. Tate had insisted that she learn how to care for it as well as shoot, since her life would come to depend on it.

She could have reached town with another fifteen or twenty minutes of riding, but she decided to stop and spend the night.

She was not the same Liz Archer who had left Newton, Kansas, months before. Too many things had happened to her, beginning with Tate, the shooting of Joe Nolan, and finally her experience in Kingdom Come. There she had learned some things about herself from Andy and from Charles Edward Taker. They taught her what it was to be a woman, and convinced her that she *was* beautiful and desirable. On her own, she had learned that she could use her beauty to her advantage, and now she was thinking that, if she had to, she could also use sex.

There were no tears when she thought about Chance or her dead family. She had taken her sorrow and her tears and hidden them deep inside of her; the only emotion she allowed herself to feel was the lust for revenge.

Liz Archer had now truly *become* Angel Eyes. Those angel eyes, though still breathtakingly beautiful, had become as cold as two solid steel bullets.

In the morning Liz saddled Blossom, but she hesitated before mounting up. It occurred to her that none of the Nolans had ever seen her before, except for Billy and Joe, and they were dead. They must have heard by now, though, that Joe, like Billy, was killed by a woman. If they were waiting for a woman to come riding into town, they'd certainly be expecting her to wear a gun.

Reluctantly, she removed her gunbelt and tucked it away in one of her saddlebags. Immediately, she felt naked without its comforting weight on her right hip.

As she lifted her foot to her stirrup she hesitated again as another thought struck her. Gingerly she touched the orange bandana around her neck, then unknotted it, slipped it off and put it in the saddlebag with the gun. Now she *really* felt naked, but there was less chance of her being recognized.

She mounted Blossom and started her toward town. If the Nolans were waiting for "Angel Eyes," they were getting Liz Archer — for now.

CHAPTER SEVENTEEN

DIABLO CITY was far from being a city, but it *was* a fair-sized town. After putting up her horse and finding the hotel, she sat in her room and tried to plan her next move. She walked to her window, which overlooked the main street, and noticed a building across the street that was painted a bright yellow and had a sign outside that proclaimed: DIABLO HOUSE OF DELIGHTS. Beneath that in smaller letters it said: "All men welcome — if you can afford it."

She knew her next move.

"I'd like to talk to the owner."

The girl who had answered the door had long dark hair, thick, sensuous lips, and was wearing a blue wrap which gaped in front, revealing a short nightgown and large, pendulous breasts which she carried proudly.

"What's it about?" she asked, looking Liz Archer up and down.

"A job."

The girl flicked her eyes over her again and then said, "Wait."

The girl closed the door in her face and she heard receding steps from inside. A few minutes later she heard angry steps approaching. It was the same girl.

"Come on," she said, opening the door wide for Liz to enter, and then slamming it behind them. "Follow me," she said, angrily leading the way.

"I'm sorry if I've inconvenienced you," Liz said, but the girl continued walking and gave no indication of having heard her apology.

She knocked on the door against the back wall of the first floor, and then opened it without waiting for a reply.

"This is Mr. Madonna," she said, indicating the man behind the desk. "He's the owner."

Liz was taken aback, but then realized what a naive assumption she had made that the owner of a bordello would have to be a woman.

"You look surprised," the man said. He was tall, slim, good-looking and in his mid-thirties.

"Okay, Randi, you can go," the man said. Randi glared at him, then turned and left, slamming the office door behind her.

"She's upset."

"Why?"

"One look at you and I know why," Madonna said, walking around his desk. He approached Liz, walked around her once, rubbing his jaw. "I sure know why."

"Let me in on it."

"Randi's my best girl," Madonna said. "Brings in more money than any other two girls."

"So why should she be mad at me?"

"You're a threat to her."

"She doesn't look like she needs to worry."

"Women are insecure creatures," he said, adding, "I don't think I have to explain that to you."

"I haven't noticed."

Madonna worked his way around in front of her again, put his hands on his hips and said, "No, I guess you haven't. You want a job?"

"Yes."

"You're hired," Madonna said in clipped tones. He marched back around his desk and said, "You'll start tonight. Have you got the right kind of clothes?"

"No."

Madonna frowned, then took out a leather wallet and removed a few bills.

"Here, get yourself what you need. Have you got a place to stay?"

"The hotel."

"If you work out I'll want you to move in here. Will that be a problem?"

"No."

"All right," he said, putting the wallet away and sitting down. "I've got some paperwork to do, so I'll see you tonight, no later than eight."

"All right," she said, tucking the money away. "Thanks, Mr. Madonna."

"Call me Steve. All the girls do. We'll get to know each other pretty well, you and I," he said, letting his gaze glide over her once again. "That's all."

He returned to his paperwork and she knew she'd been dismissed.

When she left his office she found Randi waiting, leaning against the bar smoking a cigarette. When the other woman saw her she threw the cigarette to the floor, ground it under her heel and pushed off the bar.

"You got the job." It was a statement, not a question.

"Yes."

"Then you'd better know something," Randi said. "I'm the number one girl here and everybody knows it."

"That's fine with me."

Randi seemed taken aback by the fact that Liz offered no argument. She seemed uncertain about what to do next.

"Will you introduce me to the other girls tonight, Randi?" Liz asked.

"Uh, sure," Randi said, still frowning. "Come a little early and I'll introduce you around."

"I'd appreciate it. See you later."

"Yeah, sure."

The dark-haired girl turned and watched the blonde leave. A woman who looked like that could certainly give her some competition if she wanted to. Apparently she didn't.

That puzzled an ambitious woman like Randi Perry.

Liz left the Diablo House of Delights knowing that Randi didn't understand her, but they each had their own goals and their own methods of achieving them.

Going back to her hotel she knew that her job here would be totally different from her job with Andrea Blake at Lady Louisa's. She was going to have to produce here. That meant do more than just standing around.

Working for Madonna she was sure that, sooner or later, she'd find out where the Nolans were without asking, and that was the key. She couldn't afford to let anyone in Diablo City know that she was looking for them.

And if that meant being a prostitute . . . well, she'd finally find out if Andy was right about her having the makings of a first-rate whore!

CHAPTER EIGHTEEN

AT SEVEN-THIRTY that evening Liz Archer arrived at the Diablo House of Delights wearing an appropriate dress she'd purchased with the money Madonna had given her. The woman in the dress shop guessed what the dress was for and sneered her way through the transaction, displaying her disapproval. As far as Liz was concerned, that was simply early confirmation that she was playing her part well.

She was certainly dressed for the part. The hardest thing for Liz was having to leave the Colt New Line in her room, but she didn't want to explain to anyone why she was carrying a gun. She didn't want to do anything that would draw undue attention to her.

Randi met her at the door and said, "We don't have any customers yet, so I'll introduce you around."

"How many girls do you have working here?"

"Eight. Nine now, counting you. Don't worry about trying to remember names. They'll remember you."

Randi brought Liz into a plushly furnished parlor off the saloon where the other girls were sitting around in various stages of dress — or undress. Apparently, some of them liked to display what they had openly, and wore little more than lingerie and garters. Randi, on the other hand, wore a dress with a low-cut front, revealing more than half of her huge breasts, but covering the remainder of her body adequately. Liz's dress was along the same lines, though not cut quite as low.

Randi went through the introductions rather quickly with Liz catching as many names as she could. The reaction seemed to be split in half, some of the girls welcoming her with smiles, some with frowns.

"Can a girl get something to drink around here?" Liz asked Randi.

"Sure," Randi said, leading her to a sideboard where there was a pitcher of some kind of liquid. "If you get thirsty you can have some tea. Steve doesn't want any of the girls drinking while on duty. He doesn't want us smelling like liquor. As if these liquored up cowpokes would know the difference."

"Is that the kind of business you usually get? Drunken cowboys?"

"Mostly. They're not that bad, really. Once in a while you get one that's really drunk, but if he gets abusive Steve'll have him thrown out."

"What about Steve?"

"What about him?"

"Does he ever get abusive?"

Randi studied Liz for a few moments and then said, "Give him what he wants and you won't have any problem."

"Is that what you do?"

"Usually. Listen, I don't know where you've worked before, or if you've worked for a man before, but he figures that since we work for him, he's entitled to a few privileges. Most of the girls agree and don't mind. If you're nice to him, he'll be pretty nice to you, Liz. In that respect, he's just like any other man. Speaking of which . . ." Randi said, nodding her head toward the entrance.

Liz looked that way and saw two men standing there, looking over the merchandise.

"It's time for the show to begin," Randi said. "Are you ready?"

Randi apparently didn't realize what a very good question that was.

Was she ready?

Liz took a deep breath and said, "Yeah, I'm ready."

Late that night, after the House closed, Liz went back to her hotel and took a steaming hot bath. The clerk hadn't wanted to draw it for her, but when she fluttered her eyelashes at him and lowered her shawl so he could see her breasts, he finally gave in.

She soaked in the tub for a long time with her eyes closed, trying to remember how many men she'd been with that night.

My God, she thought, I can't remember and I've only been at it for one day. How must Randi and the others take it?

She only remembered the first one and the last one. The first one had been a boy of about seventeen who was fascinated by her breasts. He stared at them, squeezed them and then finally suckled them as she moaned appreciatively. The boy had been so excited that, as he tried to insert his hugely stiff penis into her, he lost control, getting semen all over her thighs and the bed. She had assured him that she had been as excited as he, and it wasn't his fault. After ushering him out of the room she had changed the sheets and gone back downstairs.

The last one had been different. He had been a big man with a sloppy belly who had wanted to lick her first and had done so with no regard for her pleasure. After that he had entered her brutally. He pounded away for a short time, grunted and came, then left her to join his friends for more liquor.

Never once had she reached a peak herself, and she had no idea how frustrating that could be. Her body was tense, begging for release, and suddenly she found her hand down between her legs, stroking and rubbing. She thought about Chance, and how it had been with him. She rubbed slowly at first, getting increasingly faster until finally, with a dry sob, she received an orgasm, and refused to cry in its wake.

She dried off and told herself that it would be easier tomorrow, and the next day, because she had been through it once. All she had to do was close her eyes and retreat to the place where she'd hidden her tears, and wait there until it was all over. Most of the men, she found, had simple needs. They would rush back down to the saloon for whiskey afterwards. She didn't think she had spent more than ten minutes with any one of them.

Thank God, she thought, getting into bed, for small blessings.

CHAPTER NINETEEN

THE NEXT NIGHT when she reported for work Randi informed her that Madonna wanted to see her.

"Not there," Randi had called out when Liz started for the office. "In his room, the door at the very end of the hall."

Liz tried to read the dark-haired woman's eyes, but there was nothing there for her to see.

"I'll see you in a little while, then," Liz said.

"Don't count on it," Randi said, and turned and went into the parlor.

Liz went up to the second floor, down the hall and knocked on the door.

"Come in."

She opened the door, entered and was met enthusiastically by Madonna who was wearing a robe.

"Ah, Elizabeth, come in," he said, spreading his

arms wide in a welcoming gesture. "Welcome to my home."

She looked around and had never seen anything like it. The dominant color was a sort of maroon, including the robe.

"Do you like it?"

"It's . . . impressive," she said, marvelling at the expensive furnishings.

"You're wondering how I can afford all of this," he said, attempting to read her mind. "I save my money, spend it wisely and, above all, don't gamble."

"I see."

"Come, sit down and tell me how your first night was last night."

She followed him deeper into the room and it was then that she noticed the small table that was set for dinner for two.

"It was all right," she said.

"Well, you'll get a little rest tonight . . . of a sort," he said. "You'll have dinner here with me."

"What about downstairs?"

"Oh, the rest of the girls can handle that tonight. You're going to be up here with me tonight."

"The whole night?" she asked, wanting to get it clear at the start.

"Yes," he smiled. "The whole night."

Shouldn't be so bad, she thought, sitting in the chair he was holding out for her. Madonna wasn't bad looking, he was in excellent shape and he was a gentleman. At least, he had been so far.

Shouldn't be bad at all.

She learned a lot, that night.

After the delicious dinner Madonna took her to

bed. He was a very skillful lover, and he took great pride in displaying that skill.

At first as he approached her and began to put his hands on her she didn't respond. She intended to treat him as she had the other men, which meant closing her eyes and pretending she was somewhere else.

"You're very beautiful, you know," he said, sliding the dress down over her right shoulder and kissing her there.

"Thank you."

"Very beautiful," he repeated, sliding the garment off the left shoulder. He moved around in front of her and lowered the dress so that her breasts bobbed free. They were round, firm and beautifully formed.

"My God," he said, touching her pink nipples with the palms of his hands. "Truly lovely."

His touch was gentle and, despite herself, she began to respond to him. Her nipples swelled and became sensitive. He leaned forward and gently took one nipple into his mouth and suckled it while holding it in both hands, and then repeated the process on the other.

"The bed," he said, breathlessly. Obligingly she backed towards his bed, which was a large four-poster.

They sat together on the bed and he kissed her for the first time, gently prying her mouth open and probing with his tongue. At the same time he worked her dress down around her waist and began to run his hands over her back, her breasts, her belly.

"Here," he said, lifting her legs. She left them in that position while he slid the dress down her legs and off, and then did the same with her undergarments.

"Lie back."

She did so and he stood up to undress. Her eyes went to the ceiling, with intentions of staying there, but her curiosity got the better of her and she looked at him as he slid off the last of his clothing. His penis was fully erect and massive, probing at the air anxiously. His testicles seemed pendulous and heavy in their sack and swung back and forth between his legs as he joined her on the bed.

"Elizabeth, you're not very experienced, are you?" he asked, sliding his hand down her belly.

"N-no."

"You will be," he assured her, sliding a finger along her labia, "after tonight."

He kept sliding his finger along her vaginal lips, at the same time nuzzling and sucking her breasts. Her cleft began to run with moistness and suddenly he had a finger inside of her. She lifted her hips off the bed involuntarily to meet the pressure of his finger, and then he placed his thumb on her clitoris, which was erect. As he ministered to it, it began to throb and she began to moan, fastening her eyes on the ceiling.

"How does that feel?" he asked.

"Uh — all right — "

"Just all right, huh?" he asked, sliding a second finger inside of her and increasing the friction of his thumb against her swollen clitoris. "Is that all right?"

"Mmm — " she moaned, digging her teeth into her lower lip and undulating her hips against his hand.

"You didn't feel this way with any of those men last night, did you?"

"N-no."

"That's good," he told her, continuing to work on

her. "You shouldn't feel this with any of your customers, but you should feel *this* with me."

He did something inside of her and suddenly her hips were jumping off the bed uncontrollably. She hadn't even felt it coming as she had with Tate and Chance, but suddenly her body was racked by unbelievable spasms of pleasure that seemed as if they would never cease.

Later, he explained to her just what he had done and what her reaction had been. It was the first time she ever heard the word "orgasm," even though she had experienced it before, although never like *that*. In spite of her intentions *not* to feel anything with Steve Madonna, or any man, she had never felt anything like it before.

And Madonna wasn't finished.

Madonna asked Liz what she had done with her "men" the night before. When she got to the one who had wanted to "lick" her, he stopped her.

"Did you feel anything while he was licking you?"

"No," she said. "He just seemed to be licking too fast for me to feel anything, and then he just wanted to get it over with and go back to drinking."

"That's not the way to treat a woman," Madonna said. "Here, let me show you what it *should* feel like when you're with a man who knows what he's doing."

He positioned himself between her legs, spread them, and began to kiss the soft flesh of her pale thighs. Everything this man did seemed to be the *right* thing, she marvelled. What she should have done was get up off the bed and leave, but she *needed* this job in order to be in position to find the Nolans. And Steve Madonna was making her feel things she had never felt before.

Slowly, Madonna ran his tongue along her thighs to

her moist cleft, where he slowly licked her wet lips up and down, pausing to flick his tongue inside of her every so often. Liz began to moan and rotate her hips when suddenly he centered his attention on her clitoris. It was as if she had been struck by lightning. When the man had done this to her the night before she had felt nothing but distaste. Tonight, she felt pleasure that she never dreamed existed.

Madonna slid his hands beneath her so he could hold the firm cheeks of her behind in his hands, and then began to swirl his tongue around her clitoris while helping her match his tempo with her hips.

"Oh God . . ." she cried out involuntarily. This time she did feel the rush building up from deep down inside of her and suddenly he pinned her to the bed as she tried to move in response to it. Being unable to move seemed to intensify her "orgasm" to the point where she was moaning and begging him to stop . . . and begging him not to. . . .

"Now!" he said, getting up on his knees between her legs. He put one hand on the mattress on each side of her, so that she wouldn't be crushed by his weight, and then began to slide the length of his rigid penis along the lips of her vagina.

Her arms went around him and her knees tightened on his hips. He poked at her tender, sensitive opening with the bulbous head of his cock, and then with a quick flick of his hips, he was inside of her.

Once again he introduced her to pleasure she had never known before, hovering above her so that the only pressure on her was *inside* of her. He began slowly, building her to a peak, and then suddenly he was pounding away at her, as if he were trying to come out the other side. When her orgasm came this time she thought she would pass out. Then he was spurting inside her, ejaculating a steady stream that seemed endless.

While she rested he poured them some wine and explained some terms to her that she had never heard before. He told her different words that were used for a man and woman's anatomy, words he said that were fairly common of late in the east. Words like "pussy," "cock" and the term "fucking," which explained what they had just done.

"These words should be used when you're with a customer," he explained. "Tell him what a wonderful big cock he has, tell him that he makes your pussy feel as if it's on fire, *beg* him to fuck you . . ." He stopped, grinned at her expression and said, "Men respond to this, Liz. You'll see."

"Where did you learn all of this?" she asked, with honest curiosity. He was still a young man, and he seemed to have an awful lot of knowledge.

"We're not here to talk about me," he scolded her, "but this is my business, Liz, my craft. I learned it in New York, where I was born, where I've met people of all kinds, all nationalities. *I* learned and now I teach others . . . like you."

She could believe it, she thought, staring at him. She would never have thought that she could react to him as she had done that evening, even against her will.

"Some men, cowboys mostly, like we had last night, would rather drink than be with a woman," Steve Madonna explained to her. "In fact, I'm sorry I had to throw you in with them on your first night. There will be other men, however, who will want to spend an entire night with you.

Those men pay dearly for that pleasure, and you will have to be able to satisfy them."

He put his wine glass down and took hers away from her. She was sitting propped up by the pillows on the bed, holding the sheet up over her breasts. He reached for the sheet now and pulled it down, so that she was totally exposed. Her heart quickened even before he touched her.

"Have you ever used your mouth on a man?" he asked, running a finger back and forth over her breasts and nipples.

She frowned and said, "I've kissed — "

"No, no," he said. "I don't mean that. In fact, if you don't want to you don't *have* to kiss any of your customers. Most of them don't know how to do it right, anyway." Then he leaned forward and covered her mouth with his. He did things during a kiss with his lips, his tongue, his teeth, but he did them without feeling. She had the impression that he was doing all of these things with her as if he were standing alongside the bed, watching.

"No," he continued, "when I asked you if you'd ever used your mouth I meant the way I used my mouth on you . . . here," he added, touching her between her legs.

"Oh . . . no," she said, finally understanding.

"Get down between my legs," he instructed her.

"Steve — " she said, starting to protest.

"Trust me, Elizabeth," he said. "You won't have to do it very often — only on special occasions with, uh, special customers — but you *will* have to know how to do it."

Hesitantly, she did as he instructed and positioned herself between his legs.

He first made her take his testicles in her hands, gently stroking them and cupping them.

She was surprised at how heavy they were. Soon, she

was running her tongue over them and he moaned appreciatively, although she suspected that he was putting on an act for her benefit.

Later, she was running her tongue along the length of his huge erection, from base to head. It felt smooth and warm against her mouth, and not at all unpleasant.

She balked, however, when he told her to take his penis into her mouth.

"It's too big," she protested.

"Nonsense," he replied. "Your mouth is able to stretch more than you think."

"But it's too long."

"You don't have to take the whole thing, just as much as you can."

Slowly she licked the spongy head of his penis, and then allowed it to slide into her mouth. She sucked on it and used her teeth as he instructed. He told her to relax and allow a little more of his length to enter her mouth, and she did so. Eventually, she was surprised at how much of him she was able to accommodate.

"Men are all different sizes," he explained to her. "With some men you'll be able to take all of it, right down to the base. Cup my testicles now while you suck . . . yes, that's it. Now wrap one hand around the base . . . very good, yes, that's it . . . Now, when I come don't pull away."

Immediately, she started to pull away but he clamped his hand over the back of her head to keep her from doing so. He told her she'd be all right as long as she didn't panic, and above all be sure that she didn't "bite."

She continued to suckle him, because he wouldn't allow her up until she had done what he wanted, and eventually she could feel him swelling even larger within her mouth, and then he was filling her mouth and she had to remember what he said about not panicking, and not biting.

Later, he was inside of her again, pounding away at her. She felt both shame and elation and knew that she wouldn't be able to sort the two out until morning, until she could get away from him and his amazing skills as a lover.

When she woke in the morning she was exhausted.

Lying in bed staring at the ceiling it took great effort to remember where she was. The moment she did, Steve Madonna entered the room. He was wearing pants, but no shirt, and his hair was freshly damp from a bath.

"Good-morning," he greeted her.

"Um," she said. "Good-morning." She was lying spread-eagled on the bed and doubted that she could move.

"I have an early appointment," he said, "and hate to kick you out . . ."

"I'm getting up," she assured him, "as soon as I gather my strength."

"You were very good last night," he told her, pulling on a shirt. "Very good."

"Thank you," she said, remembering that this was one of the things he had "taught" her she should say to her customers after they were finished, especially the ones who stayed the entire night.

"No, I'm serious," he said, buttoning the shirt. "With a little more experience, perhaps some more lessons, you could become my top girl."

"What about Randi?"

"Randi," he said, "is twenty-eight and a cow. In another year her tits will be down to her knees. You, on the other hand, are fresh meat."

He pulled a jacket on, and said, "Think about it. Be out of here pretty soon, okay?"

"Okay."

As he left she thought over what he'd said. Randi's a cow, I'm fresh meat, and Steve Madonna is really not a very likable man.

After she dressed, still feeling weak in the legs from the countless orgasms she had experienced during the night, she left Madonna's room and met Randi in the hall. She was wearing the loose-fitting wrap again, and it was flapping open, revealing her heavy breasts.

"Leaving?"

"Yes."

"I'll walk you down."

"Suit yourself."

"How was your night?" the dark-haired girl asked. She looked at least five years older than her twenty-eight years. Calling her a "cow" had been cruel, but Liz could see that he was probably right about her, and it was a shame. She must have truly been a remarkable-looking woman a few years earlier, but her breasts, lovely and firm as they were, *had* already begun to sag.

"It was very interesting," Liz said, and Randi crossed her arms beneath those big breasts and smiled knowingly.

"He is a hell of a teacher," she said, "you have to admit that."

"I suppose so, Randi."

Randi frowned and asked, "But what?"

"He doesn't seem to be a very nice man."

"Liz," Randi said, shaking her head. "He treats his girls well, takes care of us, makes sure we don't get roughed up . . . too much. He doesn't have to be a nice man."

Randi smiled ruefully and added, ''But you're absolutely right. He's a bastard.''

''Why do you stay?''

''Where else would I go?'' Randi answered with a fatalistic shrug.

''There must be somewhere.''

''You'd better go and get some sleep, Liz,'' Randi said as they reached the front door. ''You don't look very rested.''

''It wasn't a very restful night.''

''It'll be back to work tonight, as usual,'' Randi reminded her, and Liz waved and stepped outside into the sunlight.

CHAPTER TWENTY

BACK TO WORK it was, for the next week. During that week Liz came to be accepted by the other girls, even Randi.

At the end of that week, however, Liz was starting to wonder if she could go on. She didn't know how much longer she'd be able to submit to these clumsy, groping cowboys and their "needs," while never achieving any satisfaction of her own — especially in the wake of the experience she'd had with Steve Madonna. And *he* hadn't approached her since that night. He *had* awakened a need in her, however, and it wasn't getting satisfied. Also, it was beginning to seem as if, no matter how many baths she took after a night's work, she couldn't get clean.

She started her second week in a depressed, frustrated state, which quickly changed with the arrival of two early customers.

Two mén entered Madonna's, one in his late thirties,

the other in his late teens. The older one was well over six feet tall, with broad shoulders, narrow hips, sun-burnished skin and intense eyes. The younger one was under six feet and slim, but he had the same skin and the same eyes. They had something else in common, as well. It was obvious to her that they were brothers — it was also obvious that they were Nolans. The resemblance to the dead brothers was uncanny.

"Who are they?" she asked Randi, trying not to sound too anxious about the answer.

Randi looked toward the door and a funny look came over her face.

"The big one's Les Nolan, the other one's his brother, Blue. Their father practically owns this town."

"Their father?"

Randi nodded, keeping her eyes on the two men, and said, "Gus. They come in here every once in a while, and Steve wants them treated special."

Liz remembered what Madonna had told her about certain special customers.

"Like all night?"

"If that's what they want. You won't have to worry about Les, though."

"Why not?"

Randi looked at Liz then and said, "Because he's mine." Liz realized then what the look in Randi's eyes had been — possessiveness. "He always picks me," she added, fervently, and she left Liz to approach Les Nolan.

She saw the smile on the older Nolan's face as Randi approached him. He enclosed the dark-haired girl within the circle of one powerful arm, cupping one big breast in his massive right hand, and they walked towards the steps together, apparently to go up to her room.

Liz turned her attention to the younger Nolan brother, Blue. Smaller and thinner than his older brother, she noticed the same firm jaw present in both of them. This strong jaw was, she assumed, a trait of the Nolan family.

Liz drifted over to Susie, a small, brown-haired girl with a heart-shaped face and a boyish, slim-hipped body.

"Susie, who does he usually choose?"

Susie looked over at the door, to see who she was referring to, and then said. "Oh, you mean Blue? I don't think he's ever been with the same girl twice. Since you're new, he might even pick you."

"Do we have to wait to see who he picks?"

"Hell, no. If he appeals to you, go get him. I like older men, myself." She stared wistfully up the stairs and said, "I wish his brother would pick me once. There's something about him . . ."

She was right. Liz had seen it herself. There was something magnetic about Les Nolan, possibly the fact that he was such a large, powerful man with an aura of deadliness about him. It did not appeal to her since he *was* a Nolan, but she *had* recognized it.

"I'll try the younger one."

"Tell him how great he is," Susie advised her. "He likes to be told he's a man."

"Is he?"

"I've heard that he is . . . with a gun in his hand. Without it . . ." Susie shrugged.

"Thanks."

"Sure, honey."

Liz decided to move in on Blue Nolan while he was still looking the girls over, trying to make a decision.

This would be it at last, she thought. Contact! This would make everything in the past worthwhile.

Now she could start forming a plan to bring about the end of the Nolan family!

As Liz approached, the young man moved his eyes and caught sight of her. His eyes roved over her hungrily.

"Hi," she said, giving him her best seductive look. If nothing else, she had gotten the act down perfectly during her week there.

"Howdy," he said, his eyes glued to her cleavage. "You're new."

"That's right," she said, "and you're cute."

He smiled shyly and said, "Do you really think so?"

Pleased that she had obviously played him right she said, "Definitely. The girl you pick is going to be a lucky one."

"Well, you'll get to find out," he told her, "because you're it."

"Really?" she asked, trying to look thrilled.

"Let's go to your room."

"Anything you say . . . "

"Blue," he said. "My name's Blue."

"I'm . . . Elizabeth."

She slipped her arm through his and led him up the stairs, where Les Nolan had gone with Randi only moments before.

Up in her room he took hold of her arms and kissed her. Trying not to show the revulsion she felt at the touch of his hands, his lips, she returned the kiss as ardently as she could, kissing him the way she had kissed Steve Madonna.

She would use everything she had learned from Madonna, she thought, to try and take control of the young man. The fact that he was a Nolan would repulse her, and at the same time spur her on. She undid Blue Nolan's pants.

"How old are you?" she asked, contriving to sound

breathless from lust as she took his hard penis in her hands.

"Nineteen," he said, obviously proud enough of his manhood not to have to lie and say he was older.

"Mmmm," she said, rubbing his rigid column of flesh against her cheek, "you're more man than some twice your age."

In reality his penis, even erect, was not especially large. Her mouth was able to accommodate it with ease, and it took her only a few moments to bring him to a climax.

"Mmm," she told him, "you're wonderful, Blue. Are you planning on staying all night?"

"I hadn't decided," he said, breathlessly.

"Oh, please?" she said, flicking at his now limp penis with her tongue. Madonna had told her how to bring a man back to fullness, even immediately following orgasm, and she used her hands and mouth on Blue Nolan now, bringing him back to life.

"Elizabeth . . . Jesus," he moaned.

"Please?"

"Why not?" he said finally. "Les is staying all night with Randi."

"Oh, Blue," she said, taking him in her hand and tugging him toward the bed, "thank you."

By morning Blue Nolan was exhausted and convinced that he was in love. When he left Liz's room he promised her that he'd be back that evening.

"I can't wait," she'd said, and he'd believed her. After all, he was a Nolan, wasn't he?

He met Les out front and his older brother asked, "How was your night, kid?"

"It was fantastic, Les," Blue said, rolling his eyes appreciatively. "The best!"

"Really?" Les Nolan said, looking at his little brother in surprise. He'd never seen Blue this enthusiastic after a night with one of Steve Madona's girls. "Well, which one was it?"

"Elizabeth."

"I haven't seen her," Les said. "Is she new?"

"Yep. Only here a week. She's great, Les, really great. She's tall — not as tall as me, of course — and she's got yella hair — and she's crazy about me."

"Is that a fact?" Les Nolan said, with more than just idle curiosity. "Well, little brother, aren't you the lucky one."

"You bet!"

"Let's go get the horses and get back to the ranch," Les said. "Pa's gonna have some work for us to do. That is, if you're not too tired after your big night with this new girl, Elizabeth."

Although he was exhausted Blue Nolan felt exhilarated and he said, "Hell, no. I could work all day!"

"Well, that's damn good," Les said, slamming his younger brother on the back with a massive hand in what was supposed to be a brotherly pat. "That means you can cover for me while *I* catch a nap. Randi really wrung me out last night."

Liz Archer watched from a window while the Nolan brothers walked toward the livery stable. She felt dirtier this morning than she had any of the other mornings, but damn it, it was worth it. She had young Blue Nolan right where she wanted him. A couple more nights and he'd do just about anything she asked him to do.

Naked, she stepped in front of one of the full-length mirrors that Madonna had installed in every room and examined her body. Her breasts were not as large as Randi's, but they were big, round, and firm. Slowly, she touched her pink nipples, cupping her breasts from underneath, then ran her hands down over her belly and hips, to her thighs. There was nothing sensuous in her movements. She was merely inspecting her body the way she would inspect her gun before using it. Or after.

Bending over to pick up her dress she studied her buttocks and decided that they couldn't be any higher, firmer or smoother. Putting her dress back on she wished that she could clean herself the way she cleaned her guns after firing them, but that simply wasn't possible. Not even her long, steamy baths helped.

As she left the room she saw Steve Madonna coming up the stairs.

"Liz, wait a second."

"I need a bath."

"Take it here, then," he said, putting out a hand to stop her. "I think it's time you moved your gear in here like the other girls. That'll be your room," he said, indicating the room she had just come out of.

Liz didn't answer.

"Any objections?"

"No," she said. "None."

"I understand you took care of Blue Nolan, last night," he said, changing the subject.

"That's right."

"Be nice to him, Liz," Madonna said, warningly, "and to his brother."

"His brother went with Randi."

"Les always goes with Randi," he explained, "but that could change. Be prepared to be as nice as you have to, to either of them. The Nolan name carries a lot of weight around here."

"So I've heard."

"I want you to give them everything they deserve," Madonna told her very seriously.

"Steve," Liz said, just as seriously, "you can count on it." Then she slipped past him and headed for her hotel and a bath.

After a long bath Liz collected her gear and carried it over to Madonna's House of Delights. This was no problem for her. In some ways it might end up being an advantage. For one thing, her guns would be in the same room, inside her saddlebag.

Now that she was getting close to the Nolans, that was probably best.

CHAPTER TWENTY-ONE

THE NEXT NIGHT the Nolan brothers returned and once again Les went with Randi while Blue eagerly accompanied Liz to her new room.

When Les Nolan and Randi entered her room she turned toward him and he helped her off with her clothing while fingering her large breasts. Her nipples were dark brown and large. He rubbed them back and forth while she moaned and undid his pants so she could get at that huge, pulsing part of him.

Les Nolan knew that, although Randi was a whore, she was never faking when they were together. He knew how women responded to him, and he knew that he had more than any woman could handle, although Randi had certainly come the closest.

She was on her knees now, swirling her tongue around

the bulbous head of his massive cock, hefting his heavy balls in one hand.

"Get on the bed," he ordered, and she hurried to comply. The first time he had come to her she had been slow in obeying him and he had cuffed her a few times with those big hands. She preferred it when his hands were kneading and squeezing her, so she obeyed him instantly.

He removed his clothing, revealing an almost hairless, powerful body. He had no hair on his chest or arms or legs, but did have a heavy mat of hair around his genitals. He joined her on the bed and began to suck on her stiff nipples. She reached down to wrap both hands around his long, swollen penis, and when she thought that he was going to ram it into her, finally, he pulled away.

"Les — " she said, looking at him with puzzled, slightly out-of-focus eyes. When he saw her eyes like that he knew that she was his and he could do anything he wanted with her.

In this case, he wanted to talk.

"Randi, honey," he said, taking one breast in his hand, "tell me about this new girl, Elizabeth."

"New girl . . ." Randi said, as if she hadn't quite understood what he'd said.

"There's a new girl here at the house, isn't there?" he asked. He squeezed her breast just enough to hurt her a little, and make her pay attention.

"Oh, you mean Liz."

"Yes," Les Nolan said, grinning tightly, "I mean Liz."

"Steve hired her at the beginning of last week, when she first got to town," Randi told Les, wrapping both hands around the wrist of the hand that was holding her.

"What does she look like?" Les asked. All he'd been able to get out of Blue was "blonde and wonderful."

"She's a blonde, real pretty. But not your type."

"I'll decide that," he said, cutting her off by squeezing her breast tightly again. "Blonde — " he repeated, to remind her where she was.

"As tall as me, but not as big here," she said, touching her breast. "Still, she's got a nice body and could probably go a long way, but she doesn't have the ambition some of us have."

"What is she after, then?"

"I don't know," Randi answered frowning at Les. She wondered why he was so interested in Liz, but she was not willing to risk his anger by asking why.

His curiosity about the new girl anything but satisfied, he decided to apply himself to the task at hand. He pushed Randi down onto her back, mounted her and drove his rigid pole deep into her, bringing a gasp of pain *and* pleasure from her. He cupped her buttocks in his hands and she wrapped her meaty thighs around his waist. Then the bed was jumping off the floor and the room was filled with the sound of flesh slapping against flesh and the gasping, ragged breathing of Randi Perry as Les Nolan pounded mercilessly away at her.

In another room on the same floor Blue Nolan was being controlled, while his brother was taking control.

Blue's experience with women had been confined to his visits to the Diablo House of Delights, and the other girls, from what Liz had been able to gather, had allowed him to play the aggressor. She, on the other hand, was using every trick that she had learned during her own limited, but informative, sexual experience to gain control of him. Was it possible for a man to be so easily manipulated by a woman, simply through the use of her body?

She was amazed at how easy it was.

Now as they lay together, both satisfied, she asked him about himself, his family and home, pretending envy at his answers.

"I have no family," she said, which was true. It was all she could do to keep from screaming as she added, "It must be wonderful to have family."

"I had more," he said, staring at the ceiling. "Two more brothers, but they're dead."

"I'm sorry," she lied. She was certainly anything but sorry. "How did they die?"

"We're not sure," he said. "They were shot and killed, but we're not sure by who."

Now it was he who was lying, she thought. Couldn't they admit that both Nolan brothers had been killed by a woman?

"That's terrible," she said, trying to sound conciliatory. "Tell me again about your home."

"The Big 'N'?" he asked, running his hand over one of her perfect breasts. She moaned appreciatively, while shuddering inside.

"It's big, Elizabeth, real big, and so beautiful — not as beautiful as you, though."

"You're sweet," she said, reaching up to kiss him lightly on the lips.

He went on to tell her about his father's ranch, large and well-protected, but never once did the dense buffoon offer to take her there, and she chose not to press the issue at this point in their relationship. Their third night together, maybe, but not now.

CHAPTER TWENTY-TWO

THE THIRD NIGHT proved to be a little different, though.

"You want me to what?" Gus Nolan asked his son, Les.

"I want you to keep Blue from going into town tonight," Les told his father, again.

"Well, what the hell for?"

"I can't tell you now," Les said, "but it's important."

"You goin' to that whorehouse again?" Gus asked, suspiciously.

"Yeah, Pa."

"You beatin' your little brother's time with one of them whores?"

"Sure, Pa, that's it."

Gus shook his head and said, "Beats me why you boys keep going to that place. You should find yourselves some nice girls who'll make you good wives. I only got two of you left, ya know. I want to be a grandpa before I die.''

"Sure, Pa."

"Go ahead, then," Gus said, waving Les off. "You're old enough to fend for yourself, but maybe I can talk some sense into Blue. Go ahead, then."

"Thanks, Pa. You won't be sorry."

"I'm already sorry . . ." Gus said, but Les was already on his way to town to see a certain blonde whore.

When Les Nolan entered the Diablo House of Delights he was alone, causing Liz Archer some dismay. She watched Randi trot over to the big man, and saw them engage in a heated discussion about something. Abruptly, Randi turned, glared at Liz, and stormed off as Les Nolan approached the blonde.

"Hello," Les said.

"Hi."

"My brother tells me you're really something," Les said, moving closer to her.

"Where is Blue, tonight?"

"Oh, he couldn't make it tonight, but he asked me to give you his best." Les moved closer to Liz then and added, "But I decided to give you *my* best, instead."

Liz stared at Les Nolan and began to worry. Blue seemed to be a fairly decent young man, but Les Nolan was a different story. Also, she suspected that Les would not be quite as easy to control and manipulate.

"How about it?" he asked, grabbing her by the wrists.

"You're hurting me," she said, faking a struggle.

"Oh, you can't be that easy to hurt, can you?" he asked, tightening his grip to a point where he *was* hurting her.

"What's wrong with Randi, tonight?"

"Nothing's wrong with Randi," Les said, leaning his

face so close to Liz's she could smell the tobacco on his breath. "I just want a little change tonight."

She struggled with his grip for a few moments, but quickly realized that there was nothing she could do but go with him if she hoped to keep her plan for vengeance alive.

"All right, big man," she said. "Let's go upstairs."

"I'm all yours, girlie."

He loosened his grip and she boldly led the way upstairs.

In her room she turned on him and said, "You know you've gotten Randi real mad at me."

"That's her problem," Les Nolan said. He moved close to her, grabbed her by the shoulders and said, "Come on, get those clothes off."

He pulled the dress off her shoulders, coming very close to tearing it, and pulled it down to her waist. Her firm, round breasts bobbed freely. He grabbed them with his big hands and began to knead them.

"Hey," she gasped.

"Come on, you whores love to be treated rough," he said. To illustrate his point he pushed her so hard her feet left the floor and she landed on the bed. He pulled the dress down over her legs, tossing it onto the floor.

"Listen," she said, trying to stand up, but he put his hands against her breasts and pushed her back down.

"Stay there!" he commanded. He stepped back and started taking off his own clothes.

Liz glared at Les Nolan and thought about how easy it would be for her to reach underneath the bed, take her gun out of her saddlebags and kill him while he was undressing — but she wanted all the Nolans this time. If not for that, she would have shot him dead, right there and then. She was hoping that she could get Blue Nolan to take her out to the Nolan ranch where she'd be able to kill him, Les *and* Gus at the same time, putting an end to her hunt. If she killed Les now she'd have to go on the run and wait, God knew how long, to get Blue and Gus.

She was going to have to submit to Les Nolan if she was going to keep that plan alive.

When Les had bared his torso she saw that his chest and shoulders were hairless. He removed his gunbelt and hung it on the bedpost, then took off his trousers. His genitals were surrounded by a thick, dark tangle of hair, from which his huge penis extended. He was easily three times the size of his brother.

Naked, he approached the bed, showing off his impressive physique.

"My brother was right about one thing," he said, staring down at her.

"What?"

"You *are* beautiful."

She gritted her teeth and said "So are you."

"Is that so?" he asked, grinning. "Show me."

"What?"

"Show me how beautiful you think I am," he said, and flicked his erect penis at her to indicate what he wanted.

He was larger than any man she had ever seen before, even Steve Madonna, She was afraid that she would not be able to fit him in her mouth, and was surprised when the swollen head slid right past her lips.

"Suck it," he commanded, "and suck it good."

She closed her eyes, trying to forget who she was with, and obeyed.

To her surprise, Les Nolan did not wish to spend the night, which was just as well. He had fucked her so violently that she ached all over. Now he was dressing, grinning down at her.

"How'd you like that?"

She didn't have to feign breathlessness as she answered, "That . . . was . . . wonderful."

"Yeah, you bet it was. Now that I'm done with you I'm gonna go and find Randi."

"Randi?" she asked, widening her eyes in surprise. After what they had just done?

"Sure," he said, tossing his gunbelt over his shoulder, "you don't think one woman can satisfy me, do you?"

He walked to the door, then turned and faced her with a tight grin.

"We'll be seeing each other again, Elizabeth. Real soon."

For one frozen, frightening moment she was afraid that he knew who she was. If he went for his gun, she would never have been able to reach hers, which was under the bed in her saddlebag.

He held her eyes for one last second, then opened the door and slammed it behind him.

She breathed a sigh of relief, but the fear that she had been recognized, somehow, still remained.

Les Nolan paused right outside Liz Archer's door and frowned. He was puzzled. If she was his brothers' killer, would she have been able to submit to him that way?

He went in search of Randi Perry, who needed to be taught not to get angry with him, and decided that maybe he'd visit "Elizabeth" again tomorrow night. Next time he'd make the test a little harder to pass.

Liz rose from the bed on shaky legs and, looking down at herself, realized that Les Nolan had not even bothered to remove her stockings. She walked to the corner of the room to a pitcher and basin and proceeded to wash herself between her legs with a damp cloth.

That done she walked back to the bed and sat down, feeling wrung out. She could have reached beneath the bed, brought out her gun and gone to find Les Nolan with it, but she knew she wouldn't. Everything she had endured up to this point she had endured by choice, and she wasn't going to waste it all now. Not just because she was depressed or angry at having been manhandled by the likes of Les Nolan.

Her family had been a lot worse than simply manhandled.

She picked up her dress, surprised that it had not been damaged by Les Nolan's big hands, and started to put it on to go back to work. She was suddenly overcome by a feeling of despair that drove her back to bed.

She wondered if she'd ever be able to have normal sex with a man again after these past couple of weeks. Elizabeth Archer started to cry.

PART FOUR

CHAPTER TWENTY-THREE

LIZ SPENT the bulk of the following day in her room. Keeping the door locked she took out her guns and proceeded to clean them and make sure they were in perfect working order. With any luck, she'd be using them within a day or two. Then she'd be able to leave Diablo City behind, along with Steve Madonna, and his House of Delights. And the Nolans — all dead!

Les Nolan was on his way to the barn, to talk to his father, but was intercepted by his younger brother, Blue, who walked up to him and struck him an ineffectual blow across the face.

Les put his hand to his jaw and asked, "What was that for?"

"You made Pa keep me home last night while you went to town and spent the night with Liz, didn't you?"

"I did not."

Blue frowned at his brother. Les was a lot of things — a bully and a brute — but, to his knowledge, his older brother had never lied to him.

"What?"

"I didn't spend the night with Liz, I spent the night with Randi."

"You didn't go to bed with Liz?"

"I didn't say that," Les corrected his brother. "I said I didn't spend the night with her."

"Then you did sleep with her!"

"I didn't sleep with her." Les said patiently, "I fucked her."

"You bastard," Blue said, swinging another punch.

Les caught his brother's fist in a massive paw and said, "One's enough, little brother, you don't get two."

"You bastard!" Blue shouted again, and swung the other fist. Les moved his head aside, avoiding the blow, and then yanked on the fist he was holding, pulling Blue off his feet and sending him sprawling in the dirt.

At that point Gus Nolan came out of the barn and saw his two sons, one standing over the other.

"What the hell is going on here?" he bellowed, charging over and stepping between them. He looked down at Blue and said, "Get up on your feet, boy! What's going on here?" He looked at his oldest son.

"Nothing, Pa," Les said.

"It didn't look like nothing," Gus Nolan said. He looked at his youngest son and said, "Blue?"

"Let him tell you!" Blue shouted and stalked away.

"Blue — "

"Let him go, Pa," Les said, touching Gus's shoulder. "I gotta talk to you."

"What about?"

"About what happened in Newton."

"I don't want to talk about that!" Gus Nolan said, his face clouded over with fury. He stalked back to the barn with Les following him.

"Pa, this is important."

"That's over with."

"Not while that girl is out there."

Gus turned on Les and glared at him.

"You want me to believe my sons were shot down by a girl?"

"Pa, we've been through that. Billy *was* killed by a girl. We know that. And Joe was killed by a girl."

"We don't know that it was that girl."

"Who else could it be? Pa, look, what was that girl's name?"

"I don't know."

"We don't have any idea?"

"We didn't stop for introductions, if you'll remember, Les."

"What was their family name?"

"I don't — "

"Archer, wasn't it?"

Gus stopped a moment, then said, "I think that was it."

"All right," Les said, and turned to leave.

"Whoa, son!" Gus said, grabbing Les's arm. "What's this all about? Why the fight with your brother, and why the interest in that girl's last name?"

Les turned on his father and said, "I didn't want to say anything until I was sure."

"Sure of what?"

"I think she's here."

"That girl?"

Les nodded.

"There's a new girl at Madonna's, and I think it could be her. She's been playing up to Blue."

"And that's why you wanted me to keep Blue here last night, so you could question her?"

"I didn't question her," Les said, "I figured if she hated us that much she might not be able to — "

"I don't want to hear about what you do in that place," Gus Nolan said, holding up his hand. Gus believed in vengeance — he and his sons had killed many times — but he did not believe in sex without marriage.

"All right, Pa. I'm going back tonight, though, to make sure. If it is her, I'm gonna bring her here so you can kill her."

"I don't usually hold with killin' women," Gus Nolan said, "but if this girl did kill my sons, and you can prove to me that it's her, then I'll kill her, all right. You just bring her here and I'll do it."

"I'll need you to keep Blue here again," Les said. "She's got his head so turned I don't think he'd listen to me."

"You take care of the girl," Gus Nolan told his son, "and I'll take care of your brother."

In the early evening Liz finally decided to leave her room to get some food. As she was walking from the café where she'd had dinner, she saw a wagon moving down the main street of Diablo City with a horse trailing behind. Both wagon and horse looked familiar and she stayed where she was, hoping for a glance at the driver.

When she finally saw him, her first instinct was to run out to the man, drag him down from the wagon and hug him, but she quickly stepped behind a post to make sure that he *didn't* see her. She stayed there until he had ridden out of sight, obviously headed for the livery stable.

It was Tate Gilmore driving the rig, probably the only man alive who could stir honest feelings in her.

She hurriedly crossed the street and rushed to the Diablo House of Delights. When she got inside she ran up to her room and locked the door. She walked to the bed, reached underneath for her saddlebag and removed the orange bandana that Tate had given her. Holding it tightly in her hands she crossed to the window overlooking the main street and peered out, hoping to catch a glimpse of him.

She would not, however, want *him* to see *her*. Not knowing how long he would be staying in town, or whether he'd be visiting the House of Delights, she wondered how long she'd be able to avoid him. It would only have to be long enough for her to convince Blue Nolan to take her out to the Nolan ranch first thing in the morning.

As much as she wanted to talk to Tate Gilmore, to wrap her arms around him and just *hug* him with some honest emotion, she was also afraid of him. He didn't approve of what she was doing and would probably disapprove of her methods even more. If he saw her, he would probably try to talk her out of it.

What she feared most, she thought, twisting the orange bandana tightly around her hands, was that he might succeed. She couldn't allow that.

That night every time a man walked into the place Liz kept her face hidden until she saw that it wasn't Tate. She didn't really know Tate all that well, so she had no idea whether she *should* expect him or not. He *was* a man, though, so the chances were good that he would show up there sooner or later.

The later, she thought, the better.

Finally, a man she recognized walked in, but it wasn't Tate.

It was Les Nolan.

CHAPTER TWENTY-FOUR

THE FEAR she had felt the night before, that perhaps Les Nolan knew who she was, came back as he stood in the doorway looking over the room. He was alone, which meant that Blue had once again stayed at the ranch.

When he spotted her he beckoned to her. As she crossed the room she saw Randi approach him first.

". . . of a sudden you need two women to satisfy you?" Randi was demanding as Liz came within earshot.

"Randi, you don't need another lesson, do you?"

Liz had not seen Randi all day and as the dark-haired woman's face came into view she saw what Les Nolan was talking about. The area around Randi's right eye was bruised and swollen, although she had tried to cover it with make-up.

"No, I don't," Randi said. There was a hurt look on her face until she saw Liz, when the look changed to one of hatred.

"Go on," Les said, giving her a push. "I'll see you later."

The look of hatred remained on her face as she looked back at Les and then stormed upstairs, presumably to her room.

"Do you have to do that to her?" Liz asked.

Les looked at her and said, "She loves it. All women do." He moved closer to her and took hold of her upper arm. His grip was so hard she knew that his fingers would leave bruises behind. "I told you we'd be seeing each other again, Elizabeth."

"I hadn't expected you so soon," she said, trying to pull away from his grip, unsuccessfully.

"Don't underestimate yourself," Les Nolan said. "Let's go upstairs."

"I'm waiting for someone."

"Blue isn't coming, Elizabeth," Les told her. "Let's go upstairs." He propelled her toward the steps so that she had no choice.

At that point the front door opened and Tate Gilmore stepped in, but Liz didn't know whether or not Tate had seen her. Les did not relinquish his grip until they were in her room.

"We're going to try something a little different, tonight," he told her.

"What?"

As an answer he grabbed the front of her dress and literally tore it off with deliberate force.

"Hey," she cried as her naked breasts bounced free.

He threw the front of her dress onto the floor and slapped her across the left side of the face, knocking her to the floor, stunning her.

Her head was ringing as he reached down for her, lifted

her by the arms, pushed her down on the bed and proceeded to tear off the remainder of her clothing, including her stockings.

"Yeah," he said, unbuckling his gunbelt, "something a little different. You're gonna like it."

She tried to regain her senses as Les Nolan stripped off his clothes and approached the bed, naked and huge, pulsing in anticipation.

"Turn over," he commanded.

"What — " she began, putting her hands up in front of her. "Wait!" She was trying to stall for time so that she could get her bearings back and try to deal with him, but he wasn't giving her the time she needed.

"Turn over!" he snapped again, bringing his hand down on her flat belly with a resounding slap. She yelped in pain as his hand landed with stinging force, leaving a red imprint in its wake, and then he grabbed her by the legs and forcibly turned her over.

"No," she said, as she got some inkling of what he was intending to do.

Brutally he drove his massive cock into her from behind, and as she screamed in pain she thought of her guns, out of reach beneath the bed.

Les Nolan stayed the night with Liz, during which he slept very little, preferring to stay awake and brutalize her repeatedly in one manner or another. However, as the morning light filled the room the big man had finally fallen asleep, which was what Liz had been waiting for.

Lying spread-eagled on her back, feeling totally drained, sore and despoiled, she moved her right leg, on which Les Nolan's left leg was resting, trying to free it without waking him. All during her ordeal of that night she had thought about her guns, beneath the bed and out of reach, and this was her first opportunity to reach them. Her heart was pounding and she thought that if she didn't finally reach them now her heart would burst and she would die.

She freed her leg finally, but as she slid off the bed Les Nolan's big left hand clamped down on her right arm, holding it in an iron grip.

"Where do you think you're going?" he asked, looking at her with a bemused expression. He appeared to be one of those men who was able to come immediately awake. Either that, or he'd been feigning sleep to see what she would do.

"I — " she started to say, but he tightened his grip on her arm, cutting her short and bringing tears of pain and frustration to her eyes.

"We're not finished, yet," he said, sitting up in bed and grinning at her. "What's your last name, girl?"

"What?" Liz asked, not sure she had heard right.

"What's your last name?"

He knew who she was!

In that instant she knew that she didn't have a chance of leaving that room alive, unless she could reach one of her guns with her left hand.

"Why do you want to know my last name?" she asked, reaching beneath the bed left handed, touching her saddlebags.

"Is it Archer?" he demanded. "Is that your name, bitch? You killed my brothers, didn't you?"

"I don't know what you're — "

"Answer me, damn it!" he yelled. As her hand closed over the butt of the .22 New Line she saw him start back with his right hand for his gun.

He turned his head for a moment to locate his weapon, and as he did so she came out with the New Line. Reaching across the bed, she placed the barrel against his forehead.

"That's right, Nolan," she said, her voice full of hate. "My name is Archer." She cocked the hammer back and said, "Let go of my arm."

She saw him hesitate and said, "Go ahead, reach for your gun. Give me an excuse."

For a moment she thought he would go for his gun, but his grip on her arm lessened, and then dropped.

She backed off the bed, rose shakily to her feet and said, "Now get up and move away from the gun."

He stood up, facing her, and stepped away from his gun.

"Now what?" he asked. "Are you gonna kill me here?"

"Not unless you force me to," she said, moving around to his side of the bed.

"The way I hear it you gave my brother a chance to draw and beat him."

"You'll get your chance, but not right now."

"What's next, then?"

"First we're going to get dressed."

"Are you sure?" he asked, grinning lewdly. "We could spend some more time together, you know. There are some other things I could show you."

"Turn around!" she commanded, coming very close to blowing the grin off his face. As he obeyed she took two quick steps and brought the butt of the New Line Colt down on his head with a satisfying thud that vibrated up her arm. He dropped heavily to the floor and she stared down at him, trying to regain control of herself. She was shaking all over, sore from the abuse she had taken, and sorely tempted to end it for Les Nolan right there and then. But she reminded herself that there were two other Nolans to take care of and it would be better to end it all at one time.

And that's what she was going to do. Today!

CHAPTER TWENTY-FIVE

BY THE TIME Les Nolan began to stir, Liz Archer had washed herself using the pitcher and basin on the table by the window, and had dressed and donned her gunbelt. She had tucked the Colt New Line into her belt, inside her shirt. She took Nolan's .45 from his holster and also tucked that into her belt on the outside of her shirt.

She watched the big, naked man roll over on the floor, his eyes fluttering open, and again, as when he had awakened, he appeared to become immediately aware of his surroundings. His eyes found her and pinned her with a hard stare.

"That wasn't fair."

"Get up and get dressed," she said. "I'm sick of looking at you."

"I haven't had many women tell me that," he said, climbing to his feet, showing no ill effects from the blow he'd taken to the head.

"I don't want to hear your bragging."

"I'm not bragging," he corrected her. "Just stating fact."

She was annoyed that he didn't seem to be worried at all as he dressed. She would have preferred him to be a bit more nervous.

"What do we do now?" he asked, balancing on first one foot, then the other, to pull on his boots. "We going out in the street?"

"You're going to take me to your ranch."

He stopped and stared at her, then grinned.

"I don't believe it."

"What don't you believe?"

He stood up straight and said, "If *I* had the drop on *you* that's exactly where I'd take you."

"That may be," she said, "but it's still where we're going."

"Is this what you wanted Blue to do? Take you to the ranch so you could kill us all?"

"That's right."

"Once we're all together that's going to be a little hard, you know. Why don't you just kill me now and make sure you get one of us?" he suggested.

"I want all of you."

He grinned again and said, "You've *had* all of me, Elizabeth."

"Get your hat and let's go," she ordered.

As he got his hat and moved toward the door, she kept enough room between them so that if he made a try for her she'd be able to get her gun out in time.

"You're not going to take out your gun?"

"You've got friends in this town," she said. "I don't want to tip them off to what's going on."

"Smart girl."

"Don't get any ideas, though," she added. "If you make a wrong move I'll kill you."

"I believe you."

"You'd better."

"You'd better believe what I'm saying, though, girl," Les Nolan said, his tone deadly. "Once you're on our land, you're as good as dead."

"We'll see," Liz said. "Move."

In the hall they stopped short when they saw Steve Madonna approaching from the direction of the steps. He was checking up on the girls after their night's work.

"What the hell — "

"Get out of the way, Steve," Liz told him.

"What the hell are you dressed up like that for?" he demanded, in the manner of an employer speaking to an employee.

"She's quitting, Steve boy."

"Quitting! You can't do that."

"I don't have time to play games with you, Madonna," Liz said, harshly. "Just move out of the way!"

"Better do as she says, Steve. She's crazy."

Liz decided not to argue with Les Nolan's statement. She gave him a push toward Madonna, who hurriedly stepped out of the way. She passed him warily, but he made no move toward her. She figured they had passed their only obstacle when a voice called out from behind them.

"Stop right there!"

It was Randi holding a small gun in her hand, pointed right at Liz.

"I don't know what's going on — "

"That's right, Randi, you don't," Liz said, "so put the gun down and go back to your room."

"Where are you taking Les?" she demanded.

"She's gonna kill me, Randi," Les Nolan spoke up. "Are you gonna let her do that?"

"Kill you? What for?"

"Because he's an animal, Randi," Liz said. Madonna had flattened himself against the wall to get out of the line of fire and was now watching the proceedings with an increasingly puzzled expression. "Look what he did to your face. Is that the first time he's beaten you?"

"N-no."

"And he says you love it."

"I do not! I hate it!"

"Then take a real good look at him for the first time and know what he is. He killed my whole family, Randi, and he's not going to get away with it."

She was trying to talk Randi down as quickly as she could, before Nolan could see an opening.

"Randi, if you're going to stop me you're going to have to shoot me in the back," she said. "Let's go, Nolan."

"Shoot her, Randi," Les Nolan shouted. "Go ahead and shoot her."

Liz tensed her back, waiting for the impact of a bullet that never came. As they started down the steps she heard Les Nolan grumble, "Bitch."

"Just keep walking," Liz said, breathing easier.

It was early enough that they didn't encounter anyone else on the way to the street, and once out in the street they headed for the livery, where, first removing his rifle and throwing it into the hayloft, she made him saddle both horses, and then backed him off so she could check the cinch on her saddle.

"You're careful," he said.

"Very."

She mounted up first, wincing with the pain she still felt from his abuse and watched carefully as he climbed up on his horse.

"After you," he said, and when she shook her head he smiled and started out of the livery, his confidence apparently unshaken.

As they rode out of town they were both unaware of the man who was watching them from a window in the hotel.

Tate Gilmore rubbed his jaw thoughtfully. Last night he thought he had seen Liz Archer in the whorehouse. Liz? In a whorehouse? Yesterday, Tate could hardly believe his eyes. But when he thought about it, he was positive. It was Liz all right, and her motives not very mysterious. You couldn't ride into Diablo without hearing about the Nolans, so it wasn't very hard for Tate to figure out what Liz was doing there. He had gone upstairs himself with one of the girls and had asked her who the man was that he had seen with Liz— "the blonde," he had said. When he found out it was Les Nolan, he was sure that Liz *thought* she knew what she was doing. He decided not to make his presence known to her, and not to offer her any help. What she was doing she had to do on her own, but he decided to stick around . . . just in case.

As Tate moved away from the window and reached for his gunbelt he had a feeling that Liz Archer's long hunt was about to come to an end. Even though he was aware that she had built up something of a reputation as Angel Eyes—a name he did *not* recall having given her—he was still afraid that this time she might be taking on more than she could handle. Les Nolan had a reputation with a gun, and last night in the saloon he had heard talk that Blue Nolan, the younger brother, was actually faster than Les.

Strapping on his own gun Tate left the hotel and started for the livery stable.

It was time to give his horse some exercise.

"What are you gonna do when we get there?" Les Nolan asked Liz Archer. He had been asking her questions a good portion of the way and she had not answered him once, hoping to rattle him with the silent treatment. It was work-ing the other way around, however, as Nolan's experi-ence in these kind of situations was showing.

"You're gonna be in trouble if you do that, you know?" he said. She couldn't understand how he could keep it up without showing any signs of frustration.

"Shut up!" she finally exploded. She wished she could take it back as soon as she had spoken.

"Getting nervous, huh?" Nolan asked. "Sure, little girl, you've killed at least two men, right? Well, it ain't gonna get any easier, and we sure ain't gonna make it easy for you. Blue's young and he might get nervous, but he's fast enough to make up for that. Me, I don't get nervous, and Pa's just too dumb to get scared, so that leaves you. Don't it?"

Liz had made a mistake and she knew it. But suddenly, while Les Nolan was taunting her, she went very cold and still inside, and she was not nervous any more. She'd real-ized something which made Les's taunt much easier to take, and caused her to look forward to the final show-down with less trepidation.

She wasn't going to let Les Nolan in on it, though. She'd let him keep talking until they reached the ranch and, when the time finally came for her to kill him and his family, then she'd tell him what she was feeling inside.

If that didn't affect him, nothing would.

CHAPTER TWENTY-SIX

GUS NOLAN AND HIS SON, Blue, were about to mount up to join the rest of the ranch hands — out rounding up stray cattle — when they saw two riders approaching the house. They recognized Les Nolan riding in the lead, but it took them a few moments to realize that the second rider was a woman.

"What the hell," Blue Nolan said.

"Sonofabitch!" Gus Nolan hissed in surprise.

On a hill overlooking the Nolan ranch, Tate Gilmore dismounted, took his Winchester from its holster, picked out a tree with a Y-shaped branch and anchored his rifle barrel there. Sighting down the barrel he had not yet decided which of the men to key on, but he was satisfied to be in a position to help Liz Archer, if the need arose.

He settled down to wait and watch.

Liz couldn't see Les Nolan's face as they approached his brother and father, but she could feel the smile that spread over his face, trying to lend his confidence to them.

"Elizabeth, what are you doing here . . . with him?" Blue asked, puzzled.

"I'm sorry, Blue."

"She's not what you thought she was, little brother," Les Nolan said. "She made a good whore, though, I got to give her that."

"Les, what the hell is going on?" Gus demanded. At that moment he noticed Les's empty holster and said, "Where's your gun?"

"I've got it," Liz spoke up.

"Elizabeth — "

"Maybe you better let the lady explain," Les Nolan said. Looking over his shoulder he added to Liz, "Go ahead, girlie, tell them."

Liz ignored Les Nolan and directed herself to the other two Nolans.

"You men killed my family."

"After you killed my son, Billy!" Gus Nolan snapped.

"After," she said, very deliberately, "he gunned down the boy I was supposed to marry." She realized now that Jack Marshall had been a boy and she could never imagine herself being married to him now. At that time, though, she had been in love with him.

"That was a fair fight," Gus said, although he wasn't very convincing.

"That boy had never touched a handgun in his life. It was murder. After I took my revenge, you and your sons slaughtered my entire family. I found your son, Joe, and killed him fair and square. This is where it's all going to end."

"You going to shoot us down?" asked Gus, who was not wearing a gun.

"I'm going to give you all a fair chance, like I gave Joe."

"I don't use a handgun."

"You've got your rifle," Liz said, jerking her chin at his saddle. His horse was standing right next to him and he started to reach for his rifle.

"Leave it there," she said to him. "You're close enough."

"That's not fair."

"Your boys have their guns," she said. "It'll be fair enough."

"I don't have my gun," Les Nolan spoke up.

"You will. Get off your horse."

As Les dismounted Blue Nolan took a step and said, "Elizabeth, I can't believe this. I thought you . . . had feelings for me."

Les snorted and shook his head.

"I'm sorry, Blue," she said, "but I cringed every time you touched me."

"No, that's not true!"

"It's true, little brother. If you had given me a chance to explain, you would have known all this." Les looked up at Liz and said, "We've both had her, and now she's gonna kill us all."

"Back away," Liz told Les, and he backed up until he was standing abreast his father and brother.

"Don't go for your gun yet, Blue," Liz said. "I'm going to dismount and then toss Les his gun. After he holsters it, you men can go for your guns any time."

"You're crazy," Gus said.

"She's scared, Pa," Les said.

"You're both wrong," Liz said, and now she was prepared to let them all in on what she had discovered on the trail a short time ago. She reached into her collar, her touch lingering a moment on the little Ace of Spades that Chance Taker had given her, and then she took out the orange bandana that Tate had given her, unfurled it and smoothed it out so they could see it.

"You see, at this point I have no family and nothing to live for," she told them. "I'm not crazy and I'm not scared; I just don't care if I live or die, any more. Whatever happens here . . . I win!"

For the first time she saw Les Nolan's confidence waver, and she knew that she'd already won.

She took Les Nolan's .45 from her belt and tossed it to him.

Tate Gilmore couldn't believe what he was seeing. Liz intended to take the three men on at the same time. He picked Les Nolan as his target. Les was older and more experienced, and that more than made up for any speed the younger man had on him.

On top of that, he was the biggest target down there — but Tate knew he wouldn't fire unless Liz needed him. She wouldn't have it any other way.

This was *her* play.

As he saw his .45 floating through the air to him, Les Nolan knew he could catch it and fire at the woman before she could react. But as he caught it he watched his hand return the gun to its rightful place in his holster.

He was ready.

Liz felt ice in her veins as she waited for the Nolans to make their move. My God, three men at one time! Tate Gilmore would go crazy if he knew!

She keyed on Les Nolan. She knew that the father and brother would, too. Even though he admitted that Blue was faster, Les was the experienced one. She kept her eyes on his, waiting for the slightest giveaway, watching Blue and Gus peripherally, concentrating.

She was Angel Eyes, and she had never felt more alive!

When Les Nolan finally moved it was just as Tate Gilmore had predicted. When it was right, the man facing you would seem to be moving in slow motion. She could see the pores on Les Nolan's face, the beads of perspiration running down his right cheek. She could hear the sound Blue Nolan's gun made as it slid out of his holster.

And her own speed was uncanny.

Les Nolan's gun was not yet out of his holster when her shot caught him flush in the center of his chest. She knew she had to move *quickly* now, because Blue Nolan's gun *was* out of his holster. She turned toward him just as he was squeezing off a hurried shot which went astray. Blue tried to cock the hammer on his gun and fire again, but Angel Eyes fired, her shot shattering his right shoulder. His arm went dead and his gun fell to the ground.

Gus Nolan was trying his best to get his rifle out and pointed at her, but his haste caused him to juggle the weapon. It was pointing toward the ground when Liz pointed her gun at him and cocked it. His eyes widened as he stared at her in abject terror. And then she lowered her gun.

Her senses returned to normal and she took stock of what had taken place. Les Nolan was lying on his back in the dirt, dead. Blue Nolan was down on one knee, holding his ruined right shoulder. And Gus Nolan was waiting for the hammer to fall. When it did not, he dropped to his knees in relief. His respite was only momentary. Realizing that he was still alive, his thoughts turned to his sons.

"Les is dead, Gus," Liz said, "and Blue won't ever fire a gun again. I'm leaving you with more than you left me. I'm leaving you with one son. It's over, now." She holstered her gun and said, "It's finished."

Gus Nolan rose unsteadily to his feet and moved over to cradle his only surviving son. When his arms closed around him hugging him tightly to his chest, Gus Nolan looked at Liz Archer, and said, "It's finished."

Tate Gilmore, still not believing what he had seen, but feeling a great deal of pride, mounted up and hurried back to town.

CHAPTER TWENTY-SEVEN

LIZ ARCHER only returned to Diablo City to collect her belongings. She did not even stop to say goodbye to anyone — least of all Steve Madonna. There was no one in that town who she felt she had to speak to ever again. As she was leaving she ran into Randi Perry, who had been waiting in the hall for her.

"Is he dead?" Randi asked.

"Yes."

"Good," the dark-haired girl said with feeling. "Liz, I'm sorry — "

"Don't apologize, Randi," Liz said. "It's over, and I just want to get on with my life, which is what you should do — away from here!"

"I told you once before I have nowhere else to go. It's still true."

"I don't have anywhere to go either, Randi," Liz said, "but I'm going, anyway."

"Good luck."
"Same to you."

Riding out of town she had no idea what her next destination would be. Her quest for revenge was over. What was there for her to do, now?

She became aware, as she reached the town limits, of a wagon in the road ahead of her. She rode up to it and stopped.

Tate Gilmore looked at her in silence and said, "You rushed that last shot. That's why you only hit him in the shoulder."

Angel Eyes nodded and said, "It's just as well."

He nodded.

"Mind if I tag along for a spell?" he asked.

She shrugged and said, "I'm not going anywhere in particular."

Now *he* shrugged and said, "What a coincidence; that's just where I'm going."